What was happening? *How* was this happening?

Becoming aware that her finger was still toying with the scar on his chin, Chelsea let it slide away. What on earth was she doing? She needed to step back.

But she couldn't look away, no more than she could check the impulse to rise on her tiptoes and press her mouth to his.

Aaron's mouth was a strange mix of soft and hard, and she moaned, clutching at the front of his shirt as her pulse swelled in her head. It had been over three years since she'd kissed a man and it felt strange and unfamiliar. Because it wasn't Dom. But it also felt *good* because it wasn't Dom, and she leaned into it wanting…she didn't know what.

More? Deeper? Closer?

Whatever it was, it was a moot point as Aaron broke away, taking a half step backward.

"Oh God." Her eyes flew to his face, horrified at what she'd just done. "I…" She shook her head. "I don't know what came over me. This isn't me. I'm not after…*this*. It must be the jet lag."

Dear Reader,

It's been a while since I've written a Harlequin Medical Romance novel, but it's been extra special to come back to my roots, to where this whole roller-coaster author journey began.

Gotta admit, I was worried I'd forgotten how to do this, but then Chelsea and Aaron started whispering sweet nothings in my ear and it all came rushing back. The heart-pounding medical situations, the delicious pull of "will they, won't they," the incredible backdrop and drama of the Australian Outback. It was all just there waiting to get out of my head!

I hope you enjoy this fish out of water story featuring Chelsea, who is running away from a painful past and the strictures and restraints of her present life in the UK to finally be herself. And Aaron—tough and resilient. A man of the Outback who knows what he does and doesn't want. And he definitely doesn't want to fall for an outsider.

But sometimes life has other plans, and neither Chelsea nor Aaron are immune to the whims of fate! Cue evil author laughter.

Happy reading!

Love,

Amy xxx

NURSE'S OUTBACK TEMPTATION

———

AMY ANDREWS

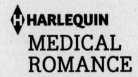

HARLEQUIN
MEDICAL
ROMANCE

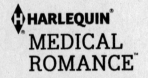

HARLEQUIN®
MEDICAL ROMANCE™

Recycling programs for this product may not exist in your area.

ISBN-13: 978-1-335-73732-8

Nurse's Outback Temptation

Copyright © 2022 by Amy Andrews

All rights reserved. No part of this book may be used or reproduced in any manner whatsoever without written permission except in the case of brief quotations embodied in critical articles and reviews.

This is a work of fiction. Names, characters, places and incidents are either the product of the author's imagination or are used fictitiously. Any resemblance to actual persons, living or dead, businesses, companies, events or locales is entirely coincidental.

For questions and comments about the quality of this book, please contact us at CustomerService@Harlequin.com.

Harlequin Enterprises ULC
22 Adelaide St. West, 41st Floor
Toronto, Ontario M5H 4E3, Canada
www.Harlequin.com

Printed in U.S.A.

my Andrews is a multi-award-winning, *USA TODAY* estselling Australian author who has written over fty contemporary romances in both the traditional nd digital markets. She loves good books, fab ood, great wine and frequent travel—preferably all our together. To keep up with her latest releases, ews, competitions and giveaways, sign up for her ewsletter—madmimi.com/signups/106526/join.

Books by Amy Andrews

Waking Up With Dr. Off-Limits
Sydney Harbor Hospital: Luca's Bad Girl
How to Mend a Broken Heart
Sydney Harbor Hospital: Evie's Bombshell
One Night She Would Never Forget
Gold Coast Angels: How to Resist Temptation
200 Harley Street: The Tortured Hero
It Happened One Night Shift
Swept Away by the Seductive Stranger
A Christmas Miracle

Visit the Author Profile page
at Harlequin.com for more titles.

I dedicate this book to Joanne Grant and Ally Blake.
I will be forever grateful for the hand-holding
and cheerleading.

CHAPTER ONE

CHELSEA TANNER WAS a puddle of sweat. Already. After three steps. The sun scorched like a blast furnace overhead and the heat danced in visible waves from the black tar of the runway. Of course, she knew that Australia was hot in November—Outback Australia even more so. And, yes, she'd checked the temperature this morning and knew it was going to be forty-one degrees when she landed in Balanora.

But knowing it and being plunged into the scalding reality of it were clearly two very different things. Because this was ridiculously hot.

Welcome to hell, hot.

Her pale skin already crackling beneath the UV, she scurried across to the modest terminal, a familiar mantra playing on repeat through her head. *It's for the best. It's for the best.* Because Christmas in England would be worse. Blessedly cool, sure, but ninth circle of hell worse, and Outback Australia was the furthest point she could travel—physically and metaphorically—from home.

So, there was no turning back and, as she stepped through the sliding doors into the frigid blast of air-conditioning, she was grateful for the lifeline, no matter the temperature.

She just needed to…acclimatise.

Expecting to find as per the email, someone waiting for her after she'd grabbed her luggage from the carousel, Chelsea glanced around. People milled and greeted, hugging and laughing as pick-ups were made, but no one appeared to be there for her.

Maybe they were just running late.

She checked her phone—no messages. Finding a set of chairs nearby, she situated herself in view of the entrance to wait. No way in hell was she doing it *outside* the terminal. After fifteen minutes had passed, however, Chelsea grabbed her phone to call the number she'd been given.

'Good afternoon, Outback Aeromedical, this is Meg, how may I help you?'

Meg sounded as peppy in real life as she had in her emails. 'Hi, Meg, this is Chelsea Tanner. I'm terribly sorry to be a bother, but I'm at the Balanora airport and I thought someone was picking me up? I can get a taxi. I just don't want to jump in one and maybe miss my lift if they're just running late.'

'*What?* But…you're not supposed to be here until Thursday.'

Chelsea frowned. 'The plane ticket you sent was for Tuesday. So…here I am.'

'Oh dear, I have it marked on the calendar as Thursday.' There was the tapping of computer keys and a clicking of a mouse in Chelsea's ear. 'I am *so* terribly sorry. I must have got my "T" days mixed up when I was inputting it to the calendar. It's absolutely no excuse, but it can get super-busy here some days and I must have been distracted. Also that whole "pregnancy brain fog" thing turns out to be very real.'

The usual tangle of emotions around pregnancy rose up but Chelsea quashed them. She was thousands of miles away from the convoluted complications of her past and Meg had already moved on.

'Gosh, this is terribly unforgiveable of me, especially after all the flight hassles you've already been through.'

Hassles was an understatement. Between the UK snap freeze, mechanical issues forcing an unscheduled landing and then, of all things, a volcanic eruption in Asia, Chelsea could have been forgiven for thinking this venture was cursed before it had even begun. And, some time during her fortieth travel hour, spent *not* in the air but in a crowded airport terminal, she had pondered whether the universe was trying to tell her something.

'You must be exhausted.'

Actually she hadn't felt too bad when she'd landed in Brisbane thirty-six hours after she was supposed to, despite not having had much sleep. Two further nights of jet-lag-interrupted sleep later, however, had not been kind. And then, with her time in Brisbane cut short thanks to her travel debacle, she'd hopped her flight to Balanora, arriving into the oven of the Outback.

As if, by just mentioning the word exhausted, Meg had made it so, Chelsea's last spark of life leached away. She certainly felt every one of her thirty-two years. 'I could sleep for a week,' Chelsea admitted.

'I bet you could!' There was more key tapping. 'Okay, stay there. I'll be right out to pick you up. Unfortunately, there's a small issue with your house. Aaron is currently staying there due to the air con in his breaking down.'

That would be Dr Aaron Vincent, Chelsea presumed, one of the senior flight doctors on the staff.

'Which is fine, it'll be fixed tomorrow, but Aaron has gone camping with some mates and won't be back until this evening. And, as he's out of mobile range, I can't call him to come and get his stuff out of your house. I mean, it's not much, but still, we like to have our houses spic and span before we hand them over, so we'll put you up in the OA room at the pub. It's permanently reserved for us in case we ever need it for stranded staff or visiting head honchos.'

Chelsea was fading fast. She didn't mind where she slept. As long as there was air-conditioning. 'Oh, thank you. That sounds great.' Once again, not the most auspicious start to her new life, but she was far too tired to care right now.

'Well, it's not the Ritz, but it's clean, safe, friendly, the water pressure is great, they serve good, hearty meals and it's air-conditioned.'

Chelsea sighed. 'You just said the magic words.'

Meg laughed. 'Hold tight, I'll be ten minutes.'

Twenty-five minutes later, Chelsea was saying goodbye to Meg as she followed a guy called Ray, who'd been serving behind the bar at the Crown hotel, up the internal stairs to the first floor. He carried her bag to the door then handed over her key.

A proper, old-fashioned key. That *slid into* a lock.

'Thank you,' she said.

He nodded and Chelsea opened the door to the massive room. Not that she noticed any of the detail. All she noticed was the general stuffiness and the giant air-conditioning unit on the wall above the bed.

Leaving her bag at the door, she crossed to the remote sitting on top of one of the bedside tables. With desperate, shaking hands, she pointed it at the unit and pressed the button labelled 'on'. For a terrible few seconds, it stuttered, whined and didn't do anything, and Chelsea thought, *Dear God, what fresh hell is this?* Then it powered to life, delivering a wave of cool air across her shoulders.

She almost collapsed on the bed in joy and relief. But not yet. Chelsea knew if she got horizontal it'd be all over, and she needed a shower. A nice, cool shower. Then she could crawl onto the bed—no, she didn't care that it was only three in the afternoon—and sleep for the next twenty-four hours.

There was nowhere to be until this time tomorrow, when Meg was picking her up to take her to her new place, so *hibernating* until then seemed like a good plan.

Adjusting the temperature on the control to the lowest possible, Chelsea snapped the heavy curtains closed over a set of French doors that opened out onto a veranda, immediately plunging the room into semi-darkness. Dragging her suitcase to the end of her bed, she grabbed clean underwear and a tank top, along with some toiletries, and headed for the shower, lingering under the spray and hoping the room would be a thousand degrees cooler when she was done.

It was, and Chelsea almost cried as she lay on the crisp, white sheet that smelled of sunshine. Her skin was cool from the shower, her hair was damp and she knew it would be ten kinds of fluff ball in the morning, but she didn't care. Right now this bed felt better than any other surface she'd ever lain on and she shut her eyes, falling head-first into the deep slumber of a person who has finally found her way through the double whammy of world time zones and militant body clocks to the deep, dark relief of unconsciousness.

Aaron Vincent was getting way too old to be drinking several nights in a row and roughing it in a swag on the hard tray of his ute, even if he'd been in the company of guys he'd known since he was a kid. Their annual camping trip out by the river that ran through Curran Downs, his family's sheep station, had been a tradition ever since they'd left school. It had survived, despite three out of the six of them not living in the area any more, and five out of the six of them being married with children.

He being the odd one out.

Luckily their wives, all women of the Outback, were understanding about this sacred time every year. Kath, Dammo's wife, who was five-and-a-half months' pregnant with their third child, called it their *knitting circle*, which they all delighted in giving him shit about.

Aaron found her affectionate description hysterical. In an area known for blokey blokes, all six of them easily fit the mould, although him probably the least. Dammo and the others were still working on the land in one form or another, whereas he'd left over a decade ago to become a doctor before finally returning, three years ago, to work with the OA.

They loved taking the piss about *soft hands* and Aaron laughed along at the jokes, but he—and they—knew he could still shear a sheep, mend a fence and gets his hands dirty as well as he ever could. And did, whenever his sister, who had largely taken over the running of the property from their father now, needed some extra help.

But he'd be lying if he didn't admit to relief as he passed the *Welcome to Balanora* sign on the way back in to town. He was looking forward to an actual mattress to cushion the twinge in his lower back. Except he stopped into the pub on his way through for a bite to eat, because he couldn't be bothered to cook anything, and Tuesdays were always roast night.

Then he got talking to three women— nurses from Adelaide—who were passing through town on an Outback road trip. They were interested in the OA, and they chatted and laughed, and it felt good to feel thirty-five instead of the seventy-five his lumbar spine currently felt. Not a bad way to spend an evening. Better than five other blokes, who hadn't showered in three days, *and* Dammo's farting dog, Kenny.

Aaron left soon after the nurses departed, only to discover his ute had a flat tyre. Too tired to do something about it or even call a cab, he turned back to the pub to enquire if the OA room was empty. When Lyle, the publican, handed over the key, Aaron decided it was a definite sign from the universe to go to bed and fix the damn tyre in the morning.

Heading up the stairs, he let himself into number seven, the blessed cool of the room only registering at the same time he yanked his shirt over his head. Frowning, he flipped on the light switch to discover he was not alone. There was a barely covered woman he didn't know in the middle of the bed, staring at him wild-eyed.

And then she screamed.

Aaron winced as she sat bolt-upright, her sandy-blonde hair in complete disarray, and dragged the sheet up to cover herself. '*Get out!* Get out *right now*!' she screeched, blinking against the flood of light. 'You come *any* closer and I will scream blue murder.'

If he hadn't been distracted by her cut-glass English accent, he'd be keen to know what colour it was she *had* screamed. 'I'm sorry, I'm sorry!' he apologised, holding out both of his hands, his T-shirt still clutched in his left hand as he backed up until his shoulder-blades hit the door.

'I didn't know anyone was in here,' he continued, keeping his voice even and low and, he hoped, reassuring. 'Lyle gave me the key.

See?' He held it up. 'It's just been a terrible misunderstanding.'

She didn't say anything as she sucked in air noisily through her flared nostrils and glared. Someone pounded on the door behind him.

'What the hell is going on in there, doc? Open up or I'll kick the bloody thing in.'

Reaching behind him slowly so as not to panic the woman with any sudden moves, he turned the door handle, stepping aside to admit Lyle. Aaron greeted the publican with a *what the hell?* expression on his face. 'You said the room was empty.'

The older man scowled at him. 'What? There's nobody in the book.'

He glanced across the room at Exhibit A, who was on her feet now and watching them both warily, the sheet wrapped tight around her, one hand clutching it close to her breast.

'Oh.' Lyle stared at her as if she'd arrived from a spaceship…because how else would anyone have got past the high-tech, triple-encrypted reservation system known as 'the book'.

Cursing under his breath, something about *bloody Ray and his testicles*, Lyle addressed her. 'I'm so sorry, m…miss.' He advanced into the room, his hands extended in some kind of apology, but her eyes grew bigger and she took a step back. Lyle halted. 'I didn't know you were here.' He looked at Aaron. 'Somebody hasn't put her in the book.'

Aaron bugged his eyes. 'Clearly.'

Lyle returned his attention to the woman who somehow managed to look haughty despite her obvious discomfort and electric-socket hair. 'Ray shouldn't have rented out this room. It's for Outback Aeromedical use only.'

'I know.' She glared, taking the haughtiness up another notch. 'I'm starting there on Friday.'

'Oh.' Aaron smiled. Now it made sense. 'You're the new nurse? Chelsea Tanner?'

'Yes.'

The team had been looking forward to her arrival this past couple of months. Having someone permanent—even if just for the year of her contract—would give some certainty and stability to the team.

If this very English miss didn't baulk at the first spider and head for home, of course.

Aaron almost walked forward to introduce himself but quashed the impulse. *Not the right time, dude. Not the right place.* She looked as if she'd been roused from a very heavy sleep, and she was a lone female, in not many clothes, confronting two strange men.

'I'm Aaron,' he said, keeping his feet firmly planted on the floor and his eyes firmly trained on her face. 'Vincent. One of the flight doctors. We…ah…weren't expecting you until Thursday?'

She huffed out an impatient breath, neither acknowledging his introduction nor answering his query. 'Yes, I know, there was a mix up with Meg, but do you think we could possibly do this introduction at a later date? Perhaps when we're both more…' She glanced pointedly at the shirt in his hand. *'Clothed.'*

Damn it! He'd forgotten he'd taken it off. Hastily, Aaron threw it back over his head. 'Of course,' he said, emerging from the neck hole and pulling the hem down. 'We'll leave you to get back to sleep.' He started to back out, elbowing Lyle, who looked as if he was still trying to fathom how his system had failed. 'Apologies again.'

'Yes,' Lyle agreed, jumping in quickly, in response to the elbow. 'Huge apologies. I'll be talking to Ray in the morning.'

She just eyed them warily as they backed out, her hand still clutching the sheet tight to her front. Easing the door gently closed, Aaron glanced at Lyle.

'I'm going to kill Ray,' he said.

Aaron might just help. 'You got another room?'

'Nope.'

Aaron sighed. Of course not. Resigned, he went and changed his tyre.

After the night's interruption had dragged Chelsea out of the deepest darkest sleep of her life she feared she wouldn't be able to get back to that place again but her fears were unfounded. It took less than a minute to slide back into that cool oblivion, ably aided by the vision of a shirtless Aaron Vincent, all six-foot-odd of broad, smooth chest, solid abs and delightfully scruffy hair.

He'd oozed *male* right across the room at her but, despite the potential threat in the situation, she hadn't felt frightened. Sure, she'd been taken by surprise and had reacted as any woman would have at finding a shirtless stranger in her room in the middle of the night, but she hadn't felt he'd had any ill intent.

On the contrary, she'd felt...*attraction*.

Maybe it was just some weird jet-lag or body clock thing. Maybe her foggy brain had been in a highly suggestible state. But, for the first time since her husband's death three years ago, things actually *stirred*. She'd been aware of him as a *man*. Not an intruder, not a threat.

A man.

And that hadn't happened for the longest time.

To make things worse, he was also the first thing she thought about when she finally awoke at two in the afternoon, which was exceedingly disconcerting. She hadn't come to Australia to meet someone, to get involved or put her heart on the line again. She'd come to start anew—*by herself.* To escape the cloying clutches of family.

Stand on her own two feet.

She'd been stuck in a rut, her wheels spinning, and it was time—past time—to start moving forward again. But to do that she'd had to leave London because to stay would have meant continuing to live a lie. Minding her words and grinding her teeth, holding back the torrent of fury that bubbled beneath the surface, until her heart had become a locked box of resentment surrounded by the brittle shell of the woman everyone wanted her to be.

The woman she used to be.

Okay, maybe flying to the other side of the

world was extreme, but she knew if she was too close to call on she'd keep being sucked back.

She needed to be out of reach.

She *needed* to be herself again, not just Dom's poor widow. *Poor Chelsea.* And she wasn't going to achieve that by mooning over some other guy. No matter how good he looked with his shirt off.

Rolling out of bed, she picked up her phone as she walked to the doors and drew back the curtains, a blast of light assaulting her eyeballs. Turning back, she grabbed a pair of shorts to go with her tank and stepped into them before scooping up her phone and heading out the glass doors.

Heat enveloped her as she stepped out onto the decking, the floorboards aged and worn beneath her feet. Placing her phone on the small round table situated not far from the doors, she continued several more feet to the gorgeous wrought-iron lace work of the railing, pleased at the full protection of the roof overhead. Squinting against the sun reflecting off metallic awnings and car roofs, she looked up and down the main street of Balanora.

It was wide, two lanes each side, with a generous section of central parking between.

The cars were mostly shaded by the huge trees planted at regular intervals down the middle. Shops lined the street on both sides, cars pulling in regularly to angle-park at the kerbs. It seemed busy, with plenty of people coming and going, and more traffic than she'd imagined.

It didn't take long for the beat of the sun to drive her back and she sat at the table, the only occupant on the long veranda as she checked her texts and emails. There were several from friends, checking she'd arrived okay, and several more had come in overnight from her mother-in-law. Chelsea had texted Francesca when she'd landed in Brisbane to let her know she'd arrived safely but hadn't responded to any of the others.

The older woman hadn't wanted her to go, had fretted that she'd be too far away from the people who loved her, but she'd eventually understood Chelsea's need to get away. Still, she wasn't above turning the screws, as the video she'd sent two hours ago of three-year-old Alfie—Dom's son—testified.

Chelsea's finger hovered over the play button. That familiar chin cleft and expression was so like his father's. She wanted to listen to that sweet voice but was tired of the emotional wrench the mere existence of Alfie always caused. Through no fault of his own, Alfie was a living embodiment of her husband's infidelity, and she was tired of pretending she was okay.

Thankfully, a text popped up on the screen, putting off the dilemma.

Hi, Chelsea, it's Charmaine.

Charmaine White was the OA director. She had interviewed Chelsea via Zoom two months ago.

Sorry about the mix-up yesterday. Meg feels awful. I'll be in the bar in an hour if you're awake. If not just call on this number when you are and I can take you over to your new place.

New place. Sounded like heaven. Chelsea hit delete on the video and walked inside.

An hour later, Chelsea was ensconced in Charmaine's Outback Aeromedical badged SUV, driving around the airport perimeter. Charmaine had suggested a tour of the base first, to which Chelsea had enthusiastically agreed. Several aged hangar buildings, languishing in the sunlight, passed by. The largest of them loomed just ahead, gleaming white, with Outback Aeromedical painted on the side along with the logo of a red plane in the middle of a giant yellow sun.

Charmaine parked in a small car park and ushered Chelsea in the front door with a swipe card. Several offices and storage rooms occupied this area and Charmaine whisked Chelsea through, introducing her to anyone she came across, before opening a door that led out to the cavernous space of the hangar proper. Chelsea looked up. The exposed internal roof struts spanned the curve of the roof almost to the ground on both sides, giving the impression of ribs caging them inside the belly of a giant beast.

Two planes sat idle, one larger than the other, both somehow managing to look small in the great yawning space.

'That's the King Air,' Charmaine said, pointing to the smaller one. 'It's a twin turbo prop. We have two in our fleet here. This one did an immunisation clinic at one of the remote communities this morning.'

Chelsea knew from the interview with Charmaine that, as well as assistance in emergency situations, the OA also offered primary care in the form of remote clinics, dealing with things such as women's health, mental health and preventative medicine, as well as routine blood tests and screening.

'The other King Air is out on a job right now but should be touching down soon. They have a range of two thousand seven hundred kilometres. They take two stretchers and three seats.'

Charmaine walked towards the larger one and Chelsea followed. 'This is the Pilatus PC-24.' The door was closed but Charmaine stroked its gleaming white flank as if it was a favoured pet. 'Isn't she beautiful?'

'She is.'

'It's only been with us for six months but already saved five lives in three separate road accidents. It can fly faster and longer, and can use a runway as short as eight hundred metres, which is a godsend out here. It takes three stretchered patients and up to two medical teams. It's like an intensive care in the air.'

Chelsea smiled at Charmaine still petting the plane. 'I imagine these are few and far between?'

'They are,' she confirmed. 'I had to lobby hard for it to be based here. But, because we're situated ideally as far as distance goes between Darwin, Adelaide and Brisbane, and we have a proportionally large amount of accidents, both car and farm, it was a no-brainer.' She sighed. 'Flies like a dream.'

'Well, in that case, I can't wait to go up in it.'

Just then an ambulance pulled into the area in front of the hangar which was now in shadow. Several people whom she'd met earlier came out from the door behind.

'ETA?' Charmaine asked a guy in maintenance overalls—Brett, maybe?—who was heading for a tractor parked just to the left on the inside wall of the hangar.

'Five.'

'C'mon, I'll introduce you to the ambos.'

Charmaine introduced her to Kaylee and Robbo, who were friendly and personable, as they discussed the details of the traumatic amputation of several fingers and partial degloving of the hand that was currently on board the King Air. The plane came into sight and a tiny trill of excitement rumbled through Chelsea's chest. Soon that would be her, flying all over the Outback, bringing help and hope to people who might otherwise find themselves in some dire situations where distance could make outcomes bleak.

This was what she'd come here for and she couldn't freaking wait.

Chelsea watched the plane grow larger and

larger, the wheels unfolding from the under-
carriage as it descended and landed smoothly
on the shimmering tarmac with barely a
screeching of the tyres.

'Perfect,' Charmaine murmured.

The plane taxied toward the hangar as
Robbo got the stretcher out of the back of
the ambulance. The moment the plane's props
stopped spinning, the paramedics started towards it. 'C'mon,' Charmaine said with a
grin. 'I'll introduce you to the crew.'

The heat was still intense but Chelsea followed her eagerly across the hot bitumen,
squinting as the sun dazzled off the metallic
fuselage of the plane. She made a note to hit
the town tomorrow and buy the best damn
pair of sunglasses Balanora had to offer.

It was that or end up with crow's feet ten-
feet deep by the end of her year.

The door opened, lowering as they approached to form stairs. A woman, who
looked about forty, in navy trousers and
a navy polo shirt with the OA logo on the
collar and *pilot* stamped in large red letters across the front, greeted them. 'Hey,'
she said. 'Looks like we got us a welcoming party.'

'Hey, Hattie,' Charmaine greeted her.
'Textbook landing as per usual.'

'That's why you pay me the big bucks,' Hattie quipped as she descended the stairs and moved out of the way for the paramedics to move the stretcher in for the patient transfer.

'Hattie, meet Chelsea. She starts officially on Friday but I'm giving her the quickie tour today.'

The older woman held out her hand, saying, 'Pleased to meet you.'

Chelsea shook the offered hand and said, 'Likewise.'

'Ready to go?'

Glancing back to the plane at the familiar voice, Chelsea's eyes met Aaron's. Standing on the top step, framed by the door of the plane behind, in navy trousers and shirt with *Flight Doctor* emblazoned on the front in block letters, a stethoscope slung casually around his neck, he looked calm and confident. His hair ruffled in the slight hot breeze as a surge of...*something* flooded her system.

Desire, she supposed. But there was something else too. A tug that didn't feel sexual, an attraction that *wasn't* sexual.

A feeling of...yearning?

'Ready when you are,' Kaylee said.

His eyes broke contact then and a pent-up breath escaped Chelsea's lungs in a rush, her body practically sagging. Holy *freaking* moly. She hoped this was just the jet-lag because this *whatever it was* was seriously inconvenient.

Maybe it was just that she went for a particular sort of man and Aaron had pinged her radar after three years of not noticing *any* man. Dom had been a combat medic, after all. Good-looking, though in a very different way from Aaron. More pretty-boy beautiful—high cheekbones, amazing eyebrows and long eyelashes that had been his mamma's pride and joy. He hadn't been as tall or as broad, and his hair had been jet-black and shiny, his skin bronzed, hinting at his Sicilian heritage.

Hattie excused herself, breaking into Chelsea's thoughts, and she forced herself to concentrate on the activity at the plane door as they unloaded the patient. It took a few minutes, the team all working as one, but the patient was soon out and on the stretcher.

He appeared to be in his fifties, one arm heavily bandaged and elevated in a sling hanging from a pole off the stretcher, the other arm sporting two IV sites. A bag of fluid was running through the cubital fossa site in the crook of his elbow and an infusion of what she assumed to be some kind of narcotic, given he didn't appear to be in any overt pain, was hooked up to the one in the back of his hand.

He was shirtless with three cardiac dots stuck to his chest and his jeans and work boots were well-worn and dust-streaked with some darker patches of blood. A woman about the same age—his wife?—her face creased with worry, stood at the head of the stretcher, her clothes and sturdy work boots also streaked in caked-on dirt, dust and some blood.

Chelsea listened with half an ear as Aaron ran through the details for the paramedics, focused more on the deep resonance of his voice, his accent, than the content of the verbal hand over. Words such as 'mangled', 'traumatic amputation' and 'morphine' registered only on a superficial level until she heard, 'Two fingers on ice in the Esky.'

Esky? Glancing across, she saw a male flight nurse hand over a small Styrofoam container she assumed was a cool box.

The report ended and Kaylee and Robbo departed with the stretcher, the patient's wife following close behind. Aaron turned back for the plane and Chelsea wondered if he was avoiding her after what had happened last night.

'Chelsea,' Charmaine said. 'This is Trent Connor, he's one of our lifers.'

Dragging her attention off Aaron, Chelsea smiled at the statuesque indigenous man in the flight-nurse shirt. He had salt-and-pepper hair, salt-and-pepper whiskers and an easy grin. Trent's level of experience had been evident from his pertinent additions to the hand over process, his quick efficiency with the equipment and procedures and his rapport with the patient and his wife. Then there'd been the synergy between him, Aaron and the paramedics which spoke of a well-oiled team and mutual respect.

'Born and raised right here on Iningai country,' he said, offering his hand. 'Thirteen years with the service next month.'

'Hi, it's lovely to meet you.' They shook hands. 'I'll be counting on you to show me the ropes.'

'Most important thing to remember is not to eat anything in the fridge labelled "Brett" if you want to live.'

'I heard that.' A voice drifted round to them from the other side of the plane.

Trent grinned. 'He puts triple chilli on everything.'

'He does.' Charmaine shuddered. 'God

alone knows what the inside of his gut must look like.'

'Still hearing you.'

Chelsea laughed. 'Duly noted.' Although she liked her food spicy too.

'When you get settled in, you should come round for dinner one night. The missus makes a deadly risotto.'

Chelsea assumed that *deadly* in this instance was a compliment and not meant in the literal sense. 'I'd love to.'

'How come I never get an invite to dinner?'

Every sense going on high alert, Chelsea glanced behind Trent to find Aaron striding across to their group, his mop of dark-brown hair blowing all around in the light breeze, the sun picking out bronzed highlights. His strong legs ate up the distance, his gait oozing self-possession.

'Because you flirt with my wife.'

'Ha,' Aaron said as he halted opposite Trent and next to Charmaine, his hand pushing his hair back off his forehead, where it had settled in haphazard disarray. 'Your wife flirts with me, buddy.'

Trent rolled his eyes. 'My wife is Irish. She flirts with *everyone*.'

Aaron laughed and Chelsea's insides gave

a funny kind of clench at the deep, rich tone. 'True. Very true.'

'And of course,' Charmaine said as Trent excused himself and headed back to the plane, 'you've already met Aaron Vincent, one of our four flight doctors on staff.'

Steeling herself to address him directly, Chelsea schooled her features. 'Yeah, we did.'

He grimaced but a smile played on a mouth that dipped on the right. Up this close, and not in a fog of panic and jet-lag, she could see more detail than last night. Such as his eyes, that were a calm kind of grey but nevertheless seemed to penetrate right to her soul.

Thrusting his hand out, he said, 'Nice to meet you properly, Chelsea, and apologies again about last night.'

Keeping her smile fixed, Chelsea pushed the awkwardness from last night aside and took his hand. 'It's fine,' she said dismissively as a pulse of awareness flashed up her arm and their gazes locked. Those grey eyes were no longer laughing but intense, as if he could feel it too. 'These things happen.'

Aaron's features were more…spare than Dom's, she realised. Up this close, it was impossible not to compare him with the only other man who'd ever caused such a visceral reaction. Dom's face had been all smooth and perfectly proportioned, where Aaron's was kind of…battered. Like a thin piece of sheet metal that had been hammered over a mould, the indents still visible as it pleated sharply over the blade of his jaw and curved over the somewhat crooked line of his nose.

There was a slight asymmetry to his face too, the right cheekbone a little lower than the left, making his right eyebrow and eye slightly out of line with their left-sided counterparts, and causing a crookedness to the right side of his mouth, giving him that lopsided smile. A tiny white vertical scar bisected his chin at the jawline.

Once again, she was overwhelmed by the pure masculine aura of him. By a tug that was almost feral in its insistence that she move closer. Panicked that she might actually act on the impulse, she dropped her hand from his grasp, only just quelling the urge to wipe her palm on her shorts to rid it of the strange pulsing sensation.

'Will the patient be transferred to a primary healthcare facility soon?' Chelsea asked him, grabbing desperately for normality.

Just two professionals talking shop. *Nothing to see here.*

'Yeah,' Aaron confirmed. 'Balanora hospital isn't equipped for major micro-surgery but he'll get X-rays and have his condition assessed properly here first. Brisbane already knows about him. They'll be sending out a retrieval team, probably in the next couple of hours. His injury is stable but the viability of the fingers makes his transfer time critical.'

'He was lucky,' she said.

'Yep. There was a fencing accident out on one of the properties around here about five years ago that severed an arm and re-sulted in a fatality when the guy bled out.' He shook his head. 'It was awful. Trent was on the flight and it was an old friend of his. Rocked the community.'

'Does that happen often? Treating people you know?'

'Reasonably often, yes. Balanora might only have a population of three thousand but we're the major centre for the surrounding districts. People from all around shop here or see a doctor here or send their kids to school here. People with kidney disease come to the hospital for dialysis, babies are born here. There are a few restaurants and a couple of churches, and popular social events are run at the town hall every month. Not to mention the OA's regular district clinics. So, yeah, pretty much everyone knows everyone.'

Chelsea nodded slowly. Aaron's voice was rich with pride and empathy, as if he understood all too well the double-edged sword of living *in* and serving the health needs *of* a small community. That wasn't something Chelsea had ever had to worry about when she'd been flying all over the UK for the last decade on medical retrievals, mostly via chopper. The area was a similar size to the one she would be covering out here but the population differential had made the possibility of actually treating someone she knew remote.

Unlike Aaron, obviously. His steady grey gaze communicated both the privilege and the burden of such situations and, for a ridiculous second, Chelsea wanted to reach over, slide a hand onto his arm and give it a squeeze.

She didn't. But it was a close call.

After what felt like a very long pause, during which no one said anything, Charmaine broke the silence. 'You ready to check out your new digs? Your boxes arrived this morning and are in the garage. Or do you want to explore some more around here?'

Chelsea jumped at the lifeline, finally breaking the sudden intensity between her and Aaron Vincent. She did *not* want to explore more—she didn't want to be anywhere near this man and his curious ability to stir her in ways she hadn't been prepared for. She was obviously going to have to deal with this soon, but for now she was happy to pretend it was a combination of jet-lag, unresolved emotional baggage and stepping outside her comfort zone. And would pray that it was a temporary aberration.

'New digs would be good. Might as well get a start on unpacking.'

'Right.' Charmaine nodded. 'Let's go.'

CHAPTER TWO

ALMOST THREE HOURS LATER, Chelsea had made some decent headway on the unpacking in her new house, situated in a modern development on the edge of town. The shady, tree-lined street with row after row of cookie-cutter houses drowsing in the Outback heat—low-set brick with neat lawns, concrete driveways and double garages—had made her smile and excitement stir in her belly as Charmaine had pulled into the drive.

It was as different from Dom's parents' detached Georgian behemoth in Hackney as was possible and she'd felt instantly lighter.

The fact she had subsidised accommodation *and* a car included in the contract—a standard OA offering to attract experienced medical professionals to the middle of nowhere—had sweetened the deal. Looking around her now, she realised the fully furnished house was a true godsend.

Chelsea hadn't packed much to bring with her—just a dozen boxes of her most precious things, a lot of them books. She'd down-sized significantly when she'd sold the mar-tial home a few months after Dom had died. Moving in with his parents had seemed like the right thing at the time, united as they'd all been in their grief. And Francesca and Roberto had needed her in those months that had followed, clinging to her as their one last connection to their beloved son.

Hell, *she'd* needed *them*.

But it had grown increasingly hard since Alfie. Well, since before him, really, but that sweet little three-year-old had been the pro-verbial last straw.

Chelsea pushed the last of the six remain-ing boxes full of her books against the far wall in the living room. She was going to need to buy a couple of book cases because, although there were a couple of wall shelves affixed above the boxes, they weren't enough.

Francesca hadn't seen the point in Chelsea taking all her books to Australia when her contract was only for a year but Chelsea had been adamant. An obsessive reader and a vo-racious re-reader, books had been her com-fort all her life. The few memories she had of her mother were of being read to by her and, in those dark days after Dom's death, she'd buried herself in fictional worlds.

Leaving them behind would have felt like a betrayal. Plus Chelsea knew that, if this job was all she hoped it would be, she wouldn't be returning to the UK.

She just hadn't the heart to tell Francesca.

But the truth was there was nothing keeping her back home. Her mother had died in a car accident when Chelsea had been four, and her father had remarried to a woman not much older than Chelsea when she'd gone off to uni in London, and they now lived in Spain. She loved her father, and she was happy for him and had visited him in Spain, but his grief had made him emotionally distant when she'd been growing up and they weren't particularly close.

There were some aunts, uncles and cousins, and of course good friends she'd made over the years, both through work and a couple of friends through Dom, but there were so many ways to correspond these days. Chelsea knew she'd be able to keep in touch. And they could come and visit, just as she would return to the UK in a few years to catch up with everyone.

Including Dom's extended English-Italian family that was big and raucous, with so many cousins and second cousins always in each other's business, Chelsea had lost count. And, of course, Alfie. But by then she'd have had time, distance and perspective, and hopefully seeing Dom's son wouldn't be such a wrench.

Francesca wouldn't like it, she knew, but hopefully over time she'd come to realise that it had been too hard for Chelsea to stay and play the role of dutiful widow when her husband hadn't been the man she'd thought he was.

Or the one his grieving mother tried to paint him as.

She understood Francesca wanting to downplay the inconvenient truth—that her son had not been a faithful husband. He was dead. A war hero. Killed in Afghanistan. But even heroes could be flawed, and Chelsea couldn't keep being a part of the cult of Saint Dom.

Her tummy rumbled. She was hungry but also tired. *Again.* How was that even possible after sleeping for twenty-three hours?

Damn you, jet-lag.

She could eat—that would help. It would give her something active to do and the sugar would perk up her system. Because she was damned if she was going to bed this early after such a long sleep. She'd be awake at three o'clock in the morning.

Of course, she didn't have any food in her fridge, so that was a problem. Charmaine had said the small local supermarket stayed open to nine, so she could go and do some shopping, even though the mere thought made her tired. Nor did leaving the air-con appeal. But it would be something to do. And if she cooked something when she got back it would help to keep her going to a more reasonable hour.

Her phone dinged. A text from Francesca.

Missing us yet?

Chelsea grimaced. She loved her mother-in-law but it was hard to miss her when she texted every five damned minutes. Putting the phone in her pocket, she went to the kitchen to grab the car keys. Her pocket buzzed and she sighed as she removed her phone and read the text.

You must be lonely all by yourself in a strange town where no one knows you.

She almost laughed out loud as she scooped the keys off the white granite top of the island bench. The fact no one knew her in Balanora made it feel as if a boulder had been lifted off her shoulders. The phone buzzed again.

You know you can always come home again if you made a mistake.

'Damn it, Francesca,' Chelsea muttered, scowling at the screen. 'Turn the record over.' Her mother-in-law had been fretting for two months over this move.

Chelsea headed for the sliding door at the end of the kitchen that lead directly into the garage and slid it back just as a knock sounded on her front door.

Who could *that* be?

She didn't know anybody. Not many people, anyway. Maybe it was a neighbour popping by with a welcome casserole, which would save her a trip to the supermarket…

Turning round, she made her way to the front door and opened it, the warmth of the evening instantly invading the screen door that was still shut. Not that she really registered the temperature or the orange streak of the sunset sky behind the head of…*not* a neighbour.

Aaron Vincent.

Looking cool and relaxed in shorts, with a

T-shirt stretched across his chest, he smiled his crooked smile and everything south of Chelsea's belly button melted into a puddle.

'I haven't eaten yet, and I took a punt that you haven't either, and thought I'd introduce you to the delights of our very good Chinese restaurant as a formal apology for last night.' He held up a loaded plastic bag.

The outline of takeaway containers confirmed the contents of the bag, as did the aroma of dim sums and honey chicken wafting in through the screen.

'I even brought you a menu for your fridge.' He held up it up in his other hand. 'Because, trust me, you're going to want one.'

Chelsea's stomach growled in response and her mouth watered like a damned sprinkler. 'You really don't have to apologise again.'

'I know but... I am *really* sorry.'

Chelsea had never known a genuinely contrite man—especially one who looked like Aaron Vincent—could be such an aphrodisiac. Bloody hell. She could *feel* her pulse surging through her veins, beating hard at her temple and neck, and throbbing between her legs.

Gah!

A little voice in her head demanded she send him away. Tell him she was too tired.

Because him just standing on her doorstep had put her body in a complete tangle. Spending time with him, just the two of them? God alone knew how she might embarrass herself and there'd been enough embarrassment between them already.

And she was hardly dressed for company. She wore frayed denim cuts-off that probably sat a bit too high on her thighs and a snug tank that moulded her chest. Although, he had seen her in just her tank and undies last night.

Her inertia must have clued him in to her indecision. 'If you're not up for company, that's fine. I'll just leave the food with you and catch up with you tomorrow.'

Tell him you're not up to company. Send him away.

'Umm…'

The phone buzzed in her hand and Chelsea was actually grateful for Francesca's timing, for once. It gave her something to do while she thought about how she could politely decline, even though her stomach was now growling loudly enough for the entire neighbourhood to hear it.

Dom would want me to look out for you. You were the love of his life.

It was precisely the worst thing Francesca could have texted in this moment. A spike of rage lanced right through Chelsea's middle as she read the text several times. The love of Dom's life… Francesca kept saying that, but *had she been*? How much had he *really* loved her? Not enough to be faithful. Not enough to honour their marriage vows. Not enough to honour *her.*

Just…not enough.

Goaded by the hypocrisy of the text, Chelsea quashed every impulse to keep Aaron Vincent at a distance and reached for the handle of the screen door. 'Sounds great, thank you. C'mon in.'

Chelsea didn't wait for him to enter, just turned and headed down the hall that led from the front door into the living area. Entering the kitchen, she placed her phone and keys on the counter and opened the cupboard above and to the right of the worktop, grabbing two plates. She wasn't thinking about what she was doing, she was just operating on autopilot, the need to lash out mixing with the irrationality of jet-lag.

When she turned around he was there, on the other side of the island, big and solid, reaching inside the bag, pulling out the containers, busying himself with lining them up next to each other and removing the lids.

'Chopsticks?' he asked, glancing at her as he brandished a pair encased in their paper wrapper, his eyes drifting to the spot where a chunk of hair had just fallen from her up-do.

Chelsea's belly did a funny shimmy and she sincerely hoped it would stop doing that some time soon. They had to work together and feeling this…caught up every time he looked at her…would not be conducive to that. But his eyes were calm and steady, his *presence* was calm and steady, and that felt like the anchor she needed right now when these unexpected feelings had her all at sea.

'I'm afraid I never quite mastered the art.' She quickly scooped the errant slice of hair up, poking it back into the mess on top before opening the draw beside her and reaching for some cutlery. 'Fork?'

'Nah.' He took the sticks out of the wrapper and separated them, drumming them against the counter top. 'I have mad chopstick skills,' he said, then promptly dropped one.

Much to her surprise, Chelsea laughed. These past three years, laughter had felt like some terrible breach of grieving protocols in a house where the laughter had died along with Dom. But, with the constraints of home thousands of miles away, it was actually liberating.

'So I see.'

She blinked, her words taking her even more by surprise. They sounded…*normal*. As if they were just two people having a normal conversation. Normal felt weird after the tension from last night and the awkwardness on the tarmac earlier. It felt weird, too, being alone with a man in her home like this, something of which she was now excruciatingly aware as they faced each other across the island.

She hadn't even known this man twenty-four hours ago.

He grinned, picking up the stick. 'I hope you don't mind, I just picked up my standard order.'

Chelsea blinked at the six containers on the island and the bag holding two dim sums and two spring rolls. 'You eat *all* this?'

'I usually make it do two nights.'

'Does this mean I'm depriving you of dinner tomorrow?'

'I'm sure I'll survive,' he said derisively. 'Now.' He held out his hand for a plate. 'What's your poison?'

Chelsea glanced at the containers, all

heavily meat-based—beef and black bean, chicken and cashew, sweet-and-sour pork and crispy duck. 'Is this a bad time to tell you I'm vegan?'

The battered plains of his face took on a startled expression. 'Oh, crap... Are you?'

For the second time tonight, she laughed. The impulse to tease him had come out of nowhere, but God, it felt *so* good to laugh... *really* laugh. 'Sorry, no, just couldn't resist.'

Placing his hand on his chest, he huffed out a laugh. 'Thank God for that! I grew up on a sheep station. I might have had to reassess our friendship.'

Friendship.

Was that why he'd come? Not just to apologise again but to establish their boundaries? Which was probably a very good thing.

There was nothing but appreciative noises and food commentary for a few minutes as they tucked into their meals, sitting on the stools on Aaron's side of the island. He was right, the food was delicious, and Chelsea knew she'd be using the Happy Sun's takeaway menu regularly.

'Want water?' she asked as she slid off her stool. 'I'm sorry I can't offer you anything else until I pick up some groceries.'

'Water is fine, thank you.'

Locating the cupboard with glasses, she grabbed two off the shelf. 'You mentioned a sheep station?' Chelsea flipped on the tap and filled a glass. 'Is that Australian for farm?'

He nodded. 'Very, very big farms, yes. Tens of thousands of square kilometres.'

Chelsea blinked. 'That *is* big.'

'Yup. Curran Downs is small comparatively. Almost four thousand square kilometres.'

Small? That was the size of an entire *county* in the UK. She knew Australia was immense but she couldn't imagine being out in the middle of all that vastness. 'Curran Downs?' Chelsea slid a glass across to him as she took her stool again. 'That's its name?'

'Yep. It's about a hundred K north of here. Dad's still out there and my sister helps him run it.'

'You have a sister?'

'Yeah. Tracey. She's two years older than me and a born farmer. Never wanted to do anything else.'

'But not you?'

'It was expected but...' He shrugged, picking up his glass of water. 'When I was fourteen, there was a bad car accident just outside our property. A tourist had had a heart attack at the wheel and ran into about the only tree within a fifty-kilometre radius. He was trapped inside and needed the Flying Doctors to get him out, and I felt so damned useless.'

He shook his head and there was a distant look in those grey eyes, as though he was back there in that day. 'They landed on the road and managed to get him out. He arrested twice after they extracted him and they had to give him CPR before they could put him in the plane. It was very…dramatic. But they saved his life that day right in front of my eyes and it was…'

His gaze came back into focus, resting on Chelsea, and she could see how much the incident had impacted him. 'Inspiring. I knew that day I wanted to do *that*.'

'And what did your dad say?'

Laughing, he said, 'My father looked at me and said, you'd better knuckle down at school, then.'

Chelsea smiled. 'You weren't a good student?'

'I did okay but I just didn't really see the point in busting my gut studying Shakespeare and advanced algebra when I was going to be running sheep all my life.'

'And what did your mum say?'

'My mother was thrilled. She never could understand why anyone wanted to live out in the middle of nowhere. She left when I was thirteen.'

'Oh… I'm sorry.'

'It's fine.' He shrugged. 'She was a city girl. My father met her when he was on a trip to Canberra in his early twenties. She was a translator working for the French consulate. They had a whirlwind courtship resulting in an unplanned pregnancy, followed by a quickie wedding at Curran Downs. Before she knew it, she had two babies under three and… It's hard out here. Isolating. If you're not born to it, if it isn't in your blood—sometimes even if it is—it can be stifling.'

Chelsea could see that. Flying in, over endless kilometres of earth so barren it could have been another planet, the remoteness had left a stark impression. It would be very lonely, Chelsea imagined, for someone who might be used to a very different kind of life.

'Not a lot of interpreter jobs going around out here,' Aaron continued. 'Particularly in the days before the Internet. She stuck it out for as long as she could before high-tailing it to Sydney but, to be honest, I don't know if she was ever that happy. Even as a kid I could sense that about her. She loved us, of course, but Mum also loves art galleries and restaurants and live theatre. She likes to throw dinner parties. She wasn't cut out for the life out here. It...*we*...weren't *enough*, you know?'

Chelsea nodded, feeling that sentiment right down to her bones. She'd never been enough for her father. Or her husband.

A wave of empathy swamped her chest and for a moment she almost reached out and touched his arm as she'd wanted to do earlier today.

Just as earlier, she didn't. 'Could she not have lived in town?'

'She did, to start with, seeing if they could make that work, but it was in the middle of a drought, and Dad couldn't leave for date nights and conjugal visits when he was hand-feeding the stock. Running a sheep station just isn't a nine-to-five job. And the closest thing to theatre in Balanora is the annual end-of-year school concert.'

Chelsea nodded. 'Was it amicable?'

'Sure, as much as these things can be.'

'Is she still in Sydney?'

He picked up a dim sum before answering, 'Melbourne now.'

'Do you see her often?'

'I saw her quite a bit when I was studying and working in Sydney, but only a couple of times since moving back home three years ago.'

'You and your sister didn't go with her?'

'We could have done, but Tracey was adamant she wasn't going anywhere.'

'And what about you?'

'A part of me wanted to go but it also felt incredibly...disloyal to leave, particularly when things were so dire with the drought. It was all hands on deck all the time.'

Chelsea nodded as she took a mouthful of crispy duck, the skin crunching to perfection. She supressed a moan as the sweetness of plum and the tang of ginger exploded across her tongue. 'But you did leave to go to uni, right?'

'Yes, four years later. To Brisbane. The drought had broken a couple of years prior and the station was in good shape. Plus, Tracey was full-time on the farm by then. I went home and helped out in holidays and, now I'm back, I usually head out there once a week on a day off.' He smiled 'Tracey always has a job for me.'

Although she'd seen him earlier in the doorway of an OA plane with a stethoscope around his neck, it wasn't that hard to imagine him in dusty jeans, a checked shirt and cowboy hat. His face had a weathered, outdoorsy quality about it and his body had a hardness and physicality to it that hinted at manual work.

Same as his hands. Currently wielding chopsticks as if he'd been born out the back of a restaurant in China town, they weren't soft or smooth. There was a toughness to them, a thickness, a couple of tiny scars over the knuckles. Like his face, they were a little banged up. Definitely not soft or smooth.

Rough.

A tiny shiver wormed its way right up Chelsea's centre thinking how those big, capable hands might feel on her belly. On her breasts. On her inner thighs.

Oh, God.

Clearly her body had no plans to stop with whatever this was any time soon. But she could hardly kick him out mid-dinner— which *he* had bought for her—because her libido was on the blink.

That was the problem, she decided—after three years in a deep freeze, her libido had decided to roar back to life. It was probably perfectly natural and normal but right now it was inconvenient. Ignoring it as best she could, she said, 'It was always your plan? To come back home?'

'Yeah, since seeing that accident. Just because I wanted something other than the station didn't mean I wanted to move to the city and forget my roots. I just wanted to serve my community in a different way.'

'I get that.'

'Except to work in any kind of Outback Flying Doctor situation I needed emergency medicine experience, so I was away from home for over a decade, working in both Sydney and Melbourne hospitals, building that experience so I could come back to Balanora.'

She detected a streak of guilt in his voice, something which Chelsea understood acutely right now. Just because something was for the best didn't make it easy to bear.

'I came home and helped when I could, usually during shearing, but it's great to be finally home for good and only a phone call away.'

For good. It sounded very final. 'You're planning on staying with the OA?'

'Absolutely.' He took a drink of water. 'I might need to occasionally go and do a few months here and there in the city to keep my skills up to date or attend a course, that kind of thing. But I *love* this place and I *love* this job. There's such variety, and yet there's a familiarity too that speaks to that fourteen-year-old, you know?'

'Yeah.' Chelsea nodded. 'I know.' She *really* did. She'd left familiarity behind and that had been scary.

But vital.

He drained his glass and set it on the counter top. 'What about you? You're a long way from home. In my experience, people come all the way out here for three reasons. They're from the area, like me.' He held up one finger. 'They're hiding.' He held up a second. 'Or they're running away.' The third finger joined the others. 'Which one are you?'

The frankness in his steady grey gaze was unnerving. This conversation had taken a sudden probing turn. 'What about adventure?' she obfuscated.

'That why you're here?'

'Sure.' She shrugged. 'Why not?' She was *totally* running away but she wasn't going to tell him that.

'A woman after an adventure won't find much in Balanora to satisfy.'

Oh, *Lordy…* Had he chosen *satisfy* deliberately? 'Are you kidding? I'm from cold, rainy England where a lot of people consider an hour's flight and half-board in Lisbon the height of adventurous. Coming to the Antipodes is like the equivalent of climbing Mount Kilimanjaro.'

He laughed. 'Maybe. But you wait until summer reaches its zenith. It'll feel more like a wrong turn than adventure.'

Chelsea paused, a spring roll halfway to her mouth. 'It gets worse than *this*?'

He laughed, and dear God… It was deep and sonorous, settling into her marrow like a sigh. 'It does. Not too late to change your mind.'

She shook her head. 'I have a year's contract which I plan to honour.'

'And after?'

It was obvious that Aaron was trying to ascertain Chelsea's intentions. She supposed that he'd probably seen a lot of people coming and going in his time when they realised all this isolation and vastness wasn't for them. *Including his mother.* So she understood. But she wasn't about to commit to what happened after her year was up—she'd be stupid to do that when she hadn't started the damn job yet.

'I don't like to plan that far ahead any more.'

'Any more?'

Chelsea shut her eyes. Damn it…that had been a slip. Before Dom had died she'd planned everything, because so much of their lives hadn't been in their control due to his military service so she'd tried to control what she could. From meal planning to holiday itineraries to the cat worming schedule—all had been noted on both her phone calendar and a big paper one on the wall.

Now, she lived from one roster to the next and tried to be more spontaneous. Dom had teased her about how rigid she was, and even three years later she wondered if that was what he'd gone looking for in other woman—spontaneity.

When she didn't answer, Aaron said, 'Charmaine mentioned you were widowed a few years ago. I'm sorry.'

His condolences were gentle and Chelsea opened her eyes to find him watching her carefully, his grey eyes soft, radiating the kind of empathy she'd felt earlier. She looked at her hands in her lap, at the white mark on her bare ring finger, the thumb of her other hand stroking over it lightly. Chelsea had taken off her wedding band on the flight to Australia. She'd thought it would be a wrench—it hadn't been.

It had been freeing.

As freeing as it had been reverting to her maiden name from Rossi. She hadn't realised how much she'd resented them both until they were gone.

'Yes.' She glanced up to find those eyes

watching the action of her thumb before they were raised to hers again. 'Thank you.'

Holding her gaze, Aaron asked, 'Do you mind me asking what happened? You don't have to answer if you'd rather not.'

'He was collateral damage,' Chelsea said. 'His unit had been engaging the enemy and one of them had been hit. He—Dom…his name was Dom—was a combat medic. It was on his fifth tour of Afghanistan. He was rendering assistance and got caught in some crossfire when the fighting changed direction. He got hit in the neck…his carotid.'

They were the facts as dispassionately as she could tell them, because thinking about him dying in the dirt of a foreign land, his life ebbing away, was always too much. She might be angry with him, his infidelities might have irrevocably damaged how she felt about him, but it didn't reduce the senseless wrench of his death.

Aaron nodded slowly. 'Nothing anyone could have done about that.'

'No.' Obviously, Aaron was used to dealing with sudden death and the people left behind, but his calm statement of fact was worth a thousand trite inanities.

'I'm truly very sorry.'

A hot spike of stupid tears pricked at the

backs of Chelsea's eyes and she blinked them back hard. There was *no way* she was going to cry in front of a guy she barely knew over something she'd already shed a million tears about.

'Thank you.' Clearing her suddenly wobbly voice, she wrenched her gaze from his and stood, picking up his empty glass of water and her half-full one. 'I'll get us some more water.'

He didn't try to stop her, for which she was grateful, and by the time she resumed her seat her emotions had been put firmly back in place. 'So, tell me about sheep,' she said as she picked up her fork to resume eating.

'Sheep?'

'Yeah. I assume you know a bit about them?'

He chuckled. 'You could say that. Yeah.'

They continued eating and he entertained her for the next fifteen minutes about sheep facts and his own personal observations about the animal in question. It didn't require a lot of input from Chelsea, and made her laugh, which helped kick any lingering emotion to the kerb. He moved onto shearing anecdotes. Somehow it wasn't a stretch to believe that Aaron could shear a sheep.

He exuded the calm capability of a man who could do anything.

Who could do *everything*. And *that* was sexy.

'I bet you're the only doctor who's actively shearing sheep in the country.'

'I don't reckon I'd be the only one, but there wouldn't be many.' He placed the chopsticks on his empty plate. 'I should also stress that, while I am a dab hand with an electric shear, I am nowhere near as fast or as accurate as the pros.'

'How long does it take them to shear a sheep?'

'About one to two minutes usually.'

Chelsea blinked. 'Holy sheep.'

He laughed. 'Elite shearers can do it in under a minute. It takes me about five minutes.'

'Wow, I'd like to see that.' Realising what she'd said, Chelsea hastened to clarify, 'I mean, the pros. Under a minute. That's gobsmacking.'

'We have a team hitting up our place at the end of the month. There are a couple of elite guys in the crew, if you want to come out and spend some time in the shearing shed?'

'Really?'

'Sure.' He picked up his plate and hers and carried them to the sink.

A tiny trill of excitement put a smile on Chelsea's face as she watched him. 'See?' she crowed. 'I've been here for a day and I'm already lining up my adventures.'

He laughed out loud, his head titled back, exposing the light brush of stubble at this throat. 'I don't know what you think happens in a shearing shed, but it's hot and dusty and full of sweaty, uncouth blokes. Nothing very exciting, and probably a bit too Australian for a genteel English woman with a posh accent.'

It was the first time Aaron had mentioned her accent. Dom had always teased her about her *hoity toity* Reading accent. But then, anything had sounded cultured next to his snappy East End accent. Raising an eyebrow, she said, 'Genteel?' Chelsea would admit to sounding posh but she was hardly a *lady*.

'The guys will think you've just stepped out of Buckingham Palace.'

Chelsea's nose wrinkled. Her accent might sound upper-class but it was far cry from plum-in-the-mouth royalty.

'I'm just saying,' he clarified. 'Look at it as a chance to experience some Aussie farm culture, *not* an adventure.'

'I see what you're doing.' She narrowed her eyes. 'You're lowering my expectations.'

He hooted out a laugh as he re-joined her on the other side of the bench. 'Absolutely. Take your expectations, divide them by two then halve them again.'

'I'm sure it'll be great.'

Shaking his head, Aaron leaned his butt against the edge of the island, not resuming his seat. It gave Chelsea a great view of his profile—the crooked line of his nose, the smooth bulge of his bicep, the flatness of his abs. 'I should get you to sign a waiver in case they damage those cute English ears with their filthy language.'

Chelsea lifted a hand to an ear reflexively, feeling the softness of another wisp of hair that had escaped her up-do. Nobody had ever complimented her *ears* before. 'If you think a nurse who's worked in emergency departments hasn't heard worse on any given Friday or Saturday night shift, then you haven't been paying attention.'

'That's true,' he conceded.

'I've been sworn at, drunkenly propositioned, *lewdly* propositioned, bled, vomited and cried on by the best of British hooligans, and I would pit them against shearers any day.'

He laughed. 'I'm sure my lot would disagree, but I've been on the receiving end of some very colourful insults from a couple of drunk Barmy Army guys a few years back, so I'm prepared to concede.'

Turning his head, he grinned at her, and Chelsea grinned back. As an emergency doctor, he'd have no doubt seen it all too, and a tiny flare of solidarity lit her chest. Their look went on a little too long, however, their smiles slowly fading. His eyes shifted to where strands of her hair kissed the side of her neck. His hands moved and she held her breath for a loaded second or two, her skin tingling beneath the heat and heaviness of his gaze.

Her pulse thudded as time slowed. Oh, God. He was going to touch her. Worse than that, she wanted him to…

CHAPTER THREE

HE DID NOT touch her. He folded his arms instead and looked away, and Chelsea released her breath, 'Not done unpacking yet, I see.' He tipped his chin at the boxes against the far wall.

Chelsea quashed the stupid tingle running up and down the side of her neck. 'Not yet. Just my books to go.'

'Books?' He glanced at her. 'You must be a serious reader if you had to bring your books with you for a year?'

Chelsea wasn't sure if he was fishing again for her future plans, so she steered clear of that pitfall. 'I am. Always have been.'

They'd been an escape from a home life where she'd often felt like an intruder on the silence and intensity of her father's grief. Inside the pages of a book, however, she could be loud, she could be adventurous. She could be free. Free to feel things she hadn't felt able to express to someone who mostly seemed to look straight through her.

He wandered over to the handful of books she'd placed on the shelves above, giving Chelsea an unfettered view of broad shoulders, firm glutes and muscular calves. Picking up her copy of *Animal Farm*, he said, 'You like the classics?'

'I like pretty much everything. Are you a reader?'

'I am. Usually non-fiction, though. Biographies and books about the history of stuff. You know, empires or buildings or political systems. Mostly on audio.'

'That's wise. They're cheaper to lug around the world and don't require bookcases. Speaking of, is there a furniture store in town where I could purchase one?'

'There's Murphy's. In the main street. They're not exactly cheap, though. Might be better to order something online and get it delivered or check out the local buy-swap-sell pages. Lots of bargains and you could get it straight away. I have a ute, if the seller can't deliver, and can give you a hand to put it together if it's a flatpack.'

She didn't know if his offer to help came from ingrained manners, Outback hospitality or something else, but she felt sure inviting Aaron into her house again wouldn't be a good idea. Not until this…jet-lag-induced crush had passed, anyway. 'Thanks. I'll check it out.'

As if to support her jet-lag theory, a feeling of overwhelming weariness hit her out of the blue and she yawned. Aaron turned in time to see it. 'God, I'm sorry. You've had a few big days, you must be exhausted.'

'It's fine,' she dismissed. Then yawned again. He quirked an eyebrow and she gave a half-laugh. 'I'm sorry. I spend the first couple of days not being able to sleep at all and now it appears I can barely stay awake.'

'Jet-lag's like that.'

Yeah. Didn't make it any easier to tolerate, though. 'It doesn't bode well for Friday.' She had a full orientation schedule the day after tomorrow and Chelsea hoped she'd be over the worst of it by then.

'That's still two sleeps away.' Aaron checked his watch. 'It's almost eight, that's not too bad. And you'll be up later tomorrow night because of the welcome dinner at the pub.'

Chelsea's heart sank at the reminder. The thought of going out and socialising, if she felt like this again tomorrow night, made her feel even wearier. But Aaron was right, being forced to stay awake and sync her clock with Aussie time was a good strategy.

He crossed back to the kitchen, the well-developed muscles of his quads far too distracting in her foggy brain. 'I'll go so you can hit the sack. A good night's sleep tonight and you'll wake up a new woman.'

She wanted to tell him she already felt like a new woman. Moving thousands of miles away from the lush green of England to the dusty dry of the Outback, far removed from the things that had defined her since Dom's death, had seen to that. But coherency of thought was getting harder and harder, plus she didn't want to invite closer scrutiny. She'd already told him far too much about herself.

'Let me help you with the leftovers first.'

Chelsea watched dumbly, her head full of cotton wool as he went round the other side of the island, opened the draw and grabbed a fork. Picking up one half-empty rice container, he forked the contents into the other half-empty rice container. 'Oh,' she said automatically. 'You don't have to do that, I can manage.'

'It's no problem.'

Working in tandem, it took a couple of minutes to rationalise the containers to three and fridge them. Aaron flicked on the tap as Chelsea shut the fridge. 'What are you doing?'

'Just going to wash up the empties.'

Chelsea shook her head. 'No need.'

'It's not a bother,' he said dismissively. 'It'll only take me a jiffy.'

'Nope.' Chelsea crossed to the sink and took the washing-up liquid out of his hand. 'Absolutely not.' She shut off the tap. 'You've done far too much already.'

'Okay, okay.' He held up his hands in surrender. 'I know when I'm not wanted.'

Chelsea rolled her eyes even as her breath caught in her throat. If only she *didn't* want him. 'No one told me the Outback Australian male was this domesticated.'

'Sure we are,' he said with a grin. 'I can even darn a sock.'

His grey eyes sparkled and, as their arms brushed together, Chelsea became aware of their closeness. Of his laughing face, the way his fringe swept sideways across his forehead and his lopsided smile. The scar on his chin.

'Where'd you get that?' she asked, turning slightly towards him as she gave in to the impulse to touch.

Her finger pressed lightly against the raised white pucker at the centre before stroking gently, absently noticing the fine prickle of whiskers. Vaguely, Chelsea was aware of the crinkle lines around his eyes receding and the husky change to his breathing as his smile faded.

'Would you believe me if I told you a knife fight?'

Chelsea laughed, glancing into the steady grey intensity of his eyes. The space around them shrunk and her breathing roughened to mimic his, her pulse a slow throb through her temples. 'Is it true?'

'Sadly, no. I tripped over a sheep when I was a kid and conked my chin on the ground.'

'Not quite as dramatic,' she admitted with a smile, her gaze roaming over his features, wondering about every deed and mishap that had resulted in the fascinating mix of imperfections that made up his face.

He smiled too, his mouth curving up, and she itched to run her finger over the crooked line of his top lip. 'Apparently, I was an exceptionally clumsy child.'

She laughed, but it didn't last long, as their gazes locked and the air between them thickened. The heat of his body, the scent of him—honey, ginger and an undernote of something sweeter—infused the air, drawing her closer. Her heart thumped almost painfully behind her rib cage.

What was happening? *How* was this happening?

Becoming aware that her finger was still toying with the scar on his chin, Chelsea let it slide away. What on earth was she doing? She needed to step back.

Step. Back.

But her finger sliding away had parted his mouth slightly and she couldn't look away, she couldn't step back. No more than she could check the impulse to rise on her tiptoes and press her mouth to his.

Aaron's mouth was a strange mix of soft and hard, and she moaned, clutching at the front of his shirt as her pulse swelled in her head. It had been over three years since she'd kissed a man and it felt strange and unfamiliar. Because it wasn't Dom. But it also felt *good* because it wasn't Dom, and she leaned into it, wanting… She didn't know what.

More? Deeper? Closer?

Whatever it was, it was a moot point, as Aaron broke away, taking a half-step backwards. Her brain saturated in a thick fog of lust, her mouth tingling wildly, it took a second for Chelsea to register the sudden loss of sensation. But awareness came back *fast* and, with it, swift recrimination.

'Oh, God.' Her eyes flew to his face, horrified at what she'd just done. At what she'd instigated. 'I am so, *so* sorry.' She shoved a hand in her hair as she took two full steps back, heat flushing up her chest and her neck. 'I...' She shook her head. 'I don't know what came over me. This isn't me. I'm not after... *this*. It must be the jet-lag.'

Why not? People had murdered other people whilst sleep-walking. Surely a random, unsolicited kiss whilst sleep deprived wasn't that much of a stretch?

He didn't say anything, just stood there staring at her, or her mouth anyway, his eyes not quite focused, his lips still parted, a thumb pressed absently against the midpoint of his bottom lip as if he was trying to commit the moment to memory or maybe... savour it? Whatever the reason, his continued silence made it worse.

'Aaron...' she said, her voice low as she twisted her non-existent wedding band. 'Please say something.' God...she was going to have to resign before she'd even started.

Francesca would be delighted.

His hand dropped from his mouth as he snapped out of his trance. 'Its fine,' he assured her with a smile.

Oh, God, *what*? It was so far from fine it was laughable. 'No.' Chelsea shook her head vigorously. 'It is *not* fine. It was…inappropriate and I've gone and buggered up our professional relationship before it's even begun. It'll feel…weird and awkward now.' She folded her arms, feeling nine kinds of idiot. 'I'm so sorry. I can see Charmaine tomorrow about backing out of my contract. I can cover until they get someone else.'

'Whoa.' Aaron gave a half-laugh as he held up both his hands in a stopping motion. 'Hold your horses. There is no need to resign. It won't feel weird or awkward. We're two adults—two professionals. I'm sure we can work together without this being a thing.'

He might not feel weird and awkward, but she sure as hell would, and she wasn't sure she'd get over it in a hurry either. Maybe he had women he'd just met try and kiss him out of the blue every other day but it was not something Chelsea did.

She cringed again, thinking about what she'd done. 'God…' She cradled her hot cheeks in her palms. 'I'm so embarrassed.'

'Have you forgotten I crashed your hotel room last night? Consider us even in the embarrassment stakes.'

The thought cheered Chelsea for about three seconds. Until she realised it wasn't the same at all. *This* hadn't been an accident.

It wasn't as if she'd tripped and her mouth had fallen onto his. It had been deliberate, if not very well thought out.

'But it…' Aaron ran a hand along the sink edge. 'Shouldn't happen again.'

Chelsea dropped her hands. Was he mad? *Of course* not. 'Oh, God, *absolutely*. That will *never* happen again. I'm not after anything like this.'

A curious, fleeting expression crossed his face that looked a lot like regret. 'It's just that… I have a—'

'Oh, no,' Chelsea interrupted, a flush of dread hitting her veins. 'You already have a girlfriend, don't you? Or a boyfriend,' she hastened to add, not wanting to presume, because *of course* there was someone out there. The man was seriously good-looking *and* a doctor.

Just then an even worse thought slunk into her brain. 'Dear God…please tell me you're not married.' He didn't wear a wedding ring but then neither had Dom.

He chuckled, and it was deep, warm and low but somehow not reassuring. 'Chelsea, relax.' He reached out a placatory hand. 'I'm single. I just have this rule… Well, not a rule, really, that sounds very formal. More like a preference, I guess, to not get involved with a woman who's not from around here—'

'Right, yes, of course,' Chelsea said, interrupting again as relief flooded her chest. 'You absolutely don't have to say any more. I totally get that.'

She imagined that being with someone—he'd definitely clarified it would be a woman—who knew intimately what it was like to live way out here so far away from anything made relationships easier. He'd lived through the consequences of how badly it could go wrong with his mother leaving.

For a moment it looked as though he *was* going to say more but he didn't. He just nodded and said, 'It really is fine, Chelsea.'

His gaze sought hers but she couldn't quite meet his. 'Okay, thank you.'

'Well.' He lightly bopped his fist on the edge of the sink. 'I'll head off now but I'll see you tomorrow night.'

Tomorrow night. God…her welcome dinner. She was going to have to sit and socialise with a bunch of new work colleagues *and* Aaron and pretend that she hadn't taken total leave of her senses and impulsively kissed him.

Damn you, jet-lag.

'Yep,' she said, her smile strained. 'I'll be there.'

'Goodnight, Chelsea,' he murmured, then

turned and walked away, disappearing round the corner into the hallway.

Chelsea didn't move for a bit, listening to the sounds of his retreating footsteps then the closing of the door. Her hands shaking, she took two steps to the sink, flicking on the tap and splashing cold water on her still hot face. That kiss and the excruciatingly awkward conversation afterwards were nothing compared to the realisation that jet-lag had little to do with what had happened and that she, in actual fact, did have a *crush* on Aaron.

Whom she would be working with and whom had made clear that, even if she decided to ditch all her reasons for coming here—none of which involved hooking up with a guy—and wanted to get into some kind of *something* with him, outsiders were not his preference.

God…how pathetically clichéd was she? Apparently starving-for-affection, widowed nurse sleazing on to sexy doctor. *Ugh.* Chelsea lowered her head, pressing her forehead against the cool edge of the stainless-steel sink.

How was she ever going to look him in the eye again?

* * *

Aaron wasn't sure what to expect from Chelsea on Thursday night. He wouldn't have been surprised if she'd made some jet-lag-related excuse and cancelled. But she hadn't. She was here with a dozen OA staff, mostly medical, although Meg, Hattie and Carl, one of the other pilots, along with Brett, had joined them too.

Not only was she here but she was having a great time, chatting away, asking and answering questions as well as laughing at Brett's terrible dad jokes. She seemed to have slotted in easily, quickly adopting the banter that the team had always enjoyed.

Probably nobody had noticed that she'd barely acknowledged him when he'd arrived and had spoken and looked at him only when necessary. But Aaron had noticed. She was obviously still feeling mortified about the kiss despite his assurances that it was fine.

That he was fine.

The truth was it had been *more* than fine. *He* had been more than fine. He'd been attracted to her from the moment he'd switched on the light in her hotel room and she'd screamed and yelled at him to get out. The gut clench he'd felt in that moment had been *visceral* and it had nothing to do with her being in her underwear. It had been the magnificence of her fire-breathing indignation and how primed she'd been to go on the attack, her eyes spitting chips of brown ice, her messy hair flying around her head with each vigorous shake.

The reaction had been the same when he'd spied her from the door of the plane yesterday, her hair in a slim pony tail flicking from side to side as she talked, fine, escaped wisps blowing around her face.

He'd known plenty of attractive women, had even slept with a few, but none of them had made his abdomen cramp tight or his heart drop a beat the second he'd laid eyes on them.

Unfortunately, the pattern had repeated when she'd opened her door to him last night. It was the closest they'd been physically since she'd arrived and, even through the mesh of the screen, he'd felt the impact of her deep in his belly. He really just should have left there and then. Handed over the food and vamoosed.

But he hadn't.

He'd been too distracted by the way her hair kept falling out of her crazy up-do, sliding against her neck, and then her phone had chimed with an incoming message of some kind and her jaw had clenched and she'd opened the door. By the time he'd noticed her frayed denim shorts and just how well her tank-top outlined her breasts, he'd been committed.

Hell, it had taken all his willpower not to straight-out ogle.

And, when she'd started talking about herself, it had been nigh on impossible to leave because he'd wanted to know all about her, this discombobulating woman from the other side of the planet holding a world of hurt in her eyes. But then of course the kiss had happened and the wheels had fallen off the wagon.

He'd been hoping that by tonight he'd be used to seeing her and the strange pitch of his belly would be no more. Apparently not. His gut had performed its now familiar clench as he'd spotted her sitting between Charmaine and Trent in a strappy green dress, her hair all loose and flowing, dangly earrings sparkling through the strands of sandy-blonde.

It was such a stupid way to feel, given she was patently still in love with her husband. She'd tried, but she hadn't been able to hide the raw emotion when she'd talked about him, her voice turning soft and husky. And then there was that very white line on the ring finger of her left hand. The ring might not be there any more but it had obviously been only a recent removal.

Why she'd kissed him was anyone's guess. Maybe he reminded her of him. *Dom*. Maybe it had been the thought of all the adventures making her reckless. Maybe it had been a long time for her and he'd been there and it'd been a weird moment.

Hell, maybe it *had* been jet-lag.

Whatever had precipitated it, reading anything into it was a dumb idea. Even leaving aside her horrified confirmation that it would *never happen again*. Oh, and the fact *she was still in love with her husband*, and she was here for a year.

One year. If she lasted that long. And then she'd be gone and he was *not* up for that.

Aaron had seen too many mates out here devastated by romances that hadn't worked because a lot of women that came from out of town weren't prepared for the *reality* of living in the Outback. They saw *Farmer Wants A Wife* on the TV and thought it was all picnics around a shady dam and bottle-feeding cute, fluffy lambs.

Thanks to his mother's desertion, Aaron had learned early to guard his heart from women who might not stick around. Especially ones who had signed a one-year contract and had been evasive about what came after. Ones who came from the lush green of a faraway country so different from the red dirt of the Outback, it might as well have been another planet.

Sure, he'd dated local women a couple of times since returning, but it was hard when the eyes of the community were watching and far too invested in the outcome and, frankly, there was zero spark. It had been much easier to indulge in occasional discreet liaisons with women who were just *passing through*. They weren't looking for love, they certainly weren't looking to stay. But a fun night of recreational sex with an Outback flight doctor?

Hell, yes.

And, until somebody came along with spark to burn, he saw no reason to change. Unfortunately, his eyes drifted to Chelsea, his belly going into its usual inconvenient tangle.

No—*not* her. *Absolutely not.*

'Trent, perhaps if you've finished pumping Chelsea for the locations of all the best pubs in London, maybe we could ask some questions too?'

Julie Dawson, another flight doctor, spoke good-naturedly and everyone laughed. She was ten years older than Aaron and had been with the OA in Balanora for six years.

'You can always rely on me to ask the important questions, Ju-Ju,' he said with grin.

Julie shook her head and switched her attention to Chelsea. 'I understand you have a lot of critical care experience.'

Chelsea rattled off her impressive CV that spanned the last twelve years and included midwifery and both neonatal and adult ICU.

'And Charmaine was saying that you did a fair bit of retrieval stuff?' Julie continued.

'Yep. I was on both the NICU and adult ICU teams. Mostly chopper retrievals, due to the shorter distances. But there was a lot of variety, which always kept it interesting.'

'What was the most interesting thing you ever went to?' Trent asked.

'A man who got his arm ripped off by a lion at a small county fair in the wilds of Berkshire.'

There was a round of gasps. 'Was he the lion tamer?' Julie asked.

'No.' Chelsea grinned. 'He was a random local who'd been dared by the lads at the pub over the road to go and pat the lion.'

Winces broke out across faces. 'I bet he was pissed!' Brett said.

'He was roaring drunk,' Chelsea confirmed, deadpan. 'Pardon the pun.'

Everyone laughed and Aaron's lungs got tight. Chelsea was charming them all. Whatever her reasons for coming to Balanora—he was sure she was running away—old Blighty's loss was their gain.

'And what about—?' Julie began.

'Enough, Ju-Ju,' Trent interrupted. 'Enough with the resumé interrogation, it's time to get down to brass tacks.' He turned to Chelsea. 'I just thought you should know that men outnumber women three to one in the district, which means you could have your pick.'

'Trent!' Charmaine said sharply.

Aaron had always admired the way Trent clomped his way through awkward moments with his huge size twelve feet. The thing was, it was surprisingly effective with patients, who magically seemed to open up about stuff, *personal* stuff, they often wouldn't disclose to a doctor.

Ignoring the warning note in Charmaine's voice, Trent continued, *'If* you were in the market for some romance. Maybe you're not ready yet, and that's fine, but I volunteer to play Cupid if you want. You just say the word, okay?'

His delivery was matter-of-fact but also

gentle, and it seemed everyone at the table held their breath, waiting for her reply. Aaron certainly was as he vacillated between wanting to thump Trent for putting Chelsea on the spot and wanting to hear her reply.

What if she indicated she *was* in the market for romance?

Chelsea smiled. 'Thanks for the offer, Trent, much appreciated. I will definitely keep that in mind.'

It was as non-committal as her response to his questions about her plans after the contract expired, but it seemed to satisfy Trent.

'How are you finding the heat?' Hattie asked, changing the subject.

Chelsea grimaced. 'Brutal.'

There was general laughter and commiseration. 'I imagine,' Hattie said, 'it's a little different to back home right now.'

'Oh, yeah.' Chelsea took another sip of her wine. 'I mean, I've been to Australia before, so I knew it was hot, but this…'

'When were you in Australia?' Renee, another flight nurse, asked.

'About fourteen years ago. I came with a girlfriend during summer break at uni. Went to Melbourne and Sydney, the reef and Uluru before flying home.'

'That's *your* summer, right?' Brett clarified. 'Our winter?'

'That's right.'

He hooted out a laugh. 'Yeah…it's not so
hot here then. None of those places would
have prepared you for the Outback in summer.'

'You know what's worse than the heat?'
Renee said. 'The flies. Sticky, black flies
buzz, buzz, buzzing around your face.'

'Shh, don't tell her that,' Charmaine joked.
'She didn't ask me about the flies.'

'It's fine,' Chelsea assured her with a grin.
'I don't scare that easily.'

Trent pulled a five dollar note out of his
wallet and placed it on the table. 'I got five
bucks that says new girl here lasts two hours
on the ground at her first job before she says
bloody flies.'

Chelsea laughed good-naturedly as five-
dollar notes piled up in the centre of the table
and everyone claimed a time. Charmaine
wrote them all out on a napkin. 'Nine days,'
Aaron said as he threw his money down.

His prediction caused a momentary pause
in the hilarity. 'Bold,' Trent murmured.

He shrugged. Aaron knew Chelsea had already been through one of the worst things
life could throw at a person and that people

put up with a lot when they were running from something. She might wilt in the heat, and for damn sure she'd probably not last the week out without getting sunburned, but the flies would probably take a little longer to get to her.

'Looks like you have a champion,' Trent announced gleefully, snatching up Aaron's money.

Aaron cringed internally. The last thing Chelsea probably wanted after last night was for attention to be drawn to them in that way, but she looked at him properly for the first time tonight with only the tiniest trace of reserve and said, 'Thank you.'

He shrugged. 'You know you *will* say it, right?'

Lifting her chin, she looked defiantly around the table and gave a deliberate little sniff. 'We'll see,' she murmured, a smile playing on her mouth, and everyone laughed.

Which was pretty much how the next couple of hours unfolded as they ate, drank, laughed and chatted through three courses in the cool comfort of the Crown Hotel. They swapped war stories about infamous OA cases over the years, while Chelsea regaled them with her stories, ranging from a ninety-one-year-old man who had fallen down a cliff while mountain-climbing to delivering a thirty-weeker in a cow barn in the middle of a snow storm.

In many ways, the two worlds were as different as night and day. Fire and ice. Feast and famine. Desert and green rolling hills. But it was the job that connected them. The people. Whether they were about as isolated as it was possible to be on the planet, or a fifteen-minute chopper ride to the closest major trauma centre, the work was the same, the mission was the same. *Saving lives.* It was what united them all, no matter where they hailed from, and Aaron felt that link—invisible yet somehow tangible—glowing strong around the table tonight.

He felt it in Chelsea too. Here or there, she was one of *them*. Even if she could barely look at him right now.

Aaron didn't see Chelsea the next day until after lunch—in the store room, of all places. He was whistling as he entered, thinking about the great morning he and Renee had spent out at a remote clinic. The sense of community at these pop-up health sites was palpable, from grandmothers with babies on their hips, to barefoot kids kicking a footy around on a spare patch of dirt while they waited for adults to finish their business, to cups of hot tea poured straight from the billy being shared around under shady trees.

It always reaffirmed why he'd wanted to return to Balanora. Why he'd put in all those years in the city. This was home. He knew he didn't have that ancient, spiritual connection that the Iningai had to their country, but he loved the landscape and the people who lived out here in a deep and abiding way that was hard to articulate.

Seeing Chelsea appear from round the end of the main shelf as the door clicked shut behind him dragged him back to the present. She was in the navy trousers and polo shirt of the OA, *Flight Nurse* stamped in fluorescent block print across her chest. Her hair was pulled back into a pony tail, she held a clipboard in one hand and one of the small wire baskets stashed just inside the door in the other.

'Oh…' Aaron pulled up short. 'Hey.'

She stopped in her tracks too, her eyes widening. 'Hey.'

'Sorry. I didn't realise you were in here.'

'Of course not,' she dismissed, but her throat bobbed and her tone was cautious as if maybe she thought he might have tracked her down here or something. Which was utterly ridiculous. He was *restocking*, for God's sake. He was in and out of this store room most days.

'I was just…' She glanced at the clipboard. 'Searching for these items.'

Aaron nodded. Familiarising themselves with the store room was one of the exercises new employees did as part of the induction day. 'Anything you can't find?'

She blinked, as if her brain had been temporarily elsewhere. 'Oh.' She stared blankly at the clipboard. 'The intra-osseous needles.'

'Around the other side, on the right, about half way, second-bottom shelf.'

'Great.' She nodded. 'Thanks.'

But she didn't move for long moments, apparently rooted to the spot, looking at something just over his shoulder. Possibly the door… 'Something else?' he prompted.

'Um…no.' She shook her head, backing up a few steps. 'Thank you,' she murmured before turning and disappearing around the corner, a pen speared through her hair just above the band of the ponytail.

Man…that had been *awkward*. They were clearly going to need to have a talk because whatever it was they were doing now was bound to be noticed. He'd give her a week and if things were still like this then he'd approach her about discussing the issue.

Turning to his hand-written list, he grabbed a basket and started to fill it with the things he needed. Restocking after using the plane was a shared responsibility and, with Renee doing the clinic paperwork, it was his turn.

It took longer than it would usually, given how excruciatingly conscious he was of every sound Chelsea was making. His body literally *hummed* with awareness.

'Okay,' came her muffled voice from the other side. 'I give in. I can't find them.'

Despite the situation, Aaron smiled to himself. He remembered how long it had taken him to find things in here in the beginning. Placing his basket down, he strode round to the other side to find Chelsea kneeling on the floor in front of the shelf, scowling at the boxes.

Aaron paused for a moment, leaning his shoulder into the edge of the end panel. 'Want me to have a boy look?' he asked, quirking an eyebrow.

She turned her scowl on him and he couldn't help it—he laughed. It was the first time she'd looked at him with no hint of what had happened between them on Wednesday night and it was such a bloody relief.

'They're *not* here.'

Shaking his head, he pushed off the shelf and, as if she realised he was going to be almost on top of her within a few paces, she scrambled to her feet, the wariness back again.

Oh, well…it had been nice while it lasted.

As further proof the unguarded moment was over, she stepped back a couple of paces as Aaron approached. He refused to let it bother him as he stopped in front of the shelf in question, leaned down and reached for where he knew the box was stashed.

After three years, Aaron knew where *everything* lived in this store room. But the box he pulled out was full of ten millilitre syringes. Frowning, he pushed the basket she'd left on the floor aside with his foot and crouched to inspect the other boxes but Chelsea was right. It wasn't there. He checked behind the boxes at the front and the shelf below and above, in case they'd accidentally been put in the wrong place.

'Hmm,' he said, turning to face her.

Clipboard clutched to her chest, she folded her arms. 'I don't like to be the one to say I told you so, but…'

Aaron chuckled. She was looking at him again and, if he wasn't very much mistaken, there was smugness in those big brown eyes. 'I know we recently had some on order but they arrived this week, I thought.'

Intra-osseous needles—special venous-access devices that screwed into the bone, allowing use of the marrow to deliver emergency fluids when no veins could be found—weren't required that often and tended to expire before they were ever used.

'Maybe the box was removed before the replacement came in for some reason,' Aaron mused out loud. Or Tully, who took care of stores, could have been interrupted in the middle of sorting the stock that had arrived on Wednesday and not managed to get back to it yet.

Moving around Chelsea, Aaron headed for a desk area at the end and to the left where the inventory came in and was checked off before being put away. Grabbing the box cutter that lived on the desk top, he sliced several boxes open before he found what he was looking for. 'Found them,' he called, grabbing a smaller box and returning to Chelsea.

She averted her gaze as Aaron strode towards her then crouched to put the box on the shelf where it belonged. Grabbing one, he rose and handed it to Chelsea.

'Thank you,' she murmured, glancing at him briefly as she took it.

Dropping her gaze, she pulled the pen out from her hair and made a tick mark on the form clipped to the board. Rationally, Aaron knew she wasn't doing it as a turn-on but, bloody hell, something about it or about the unselfconscious way she'd done it was super-sexy, and the urge to kiss her throbbed through every cell in his body.

And he really needed to quash that urge right now because, if that was where she always stashed her pen, he was going to see that a lot, and wanting to kiss her every time she did it would be seriously inconvenient.

'Any time,' he said gruffly. 'Anything else?'

She looked at him briefly and opened her mouth, as if she was going to say something then thought better of it, and shook her head, dropping her gaze to the clipboard again.

Aaron sighed. Okay, maybe *the talk* couldn't wait a week. Maybe they should hash it out now. Staring at her downcast head, he said, 'Chelsea... I think we need to talk.'

It took a beat or two, the only sound the low hum of the air-con before there was a definite rough release of breath and her chin lifted, her gaze meeting his. 'Okay.'

'We can't keep doing this…' He waved a finger back and forth between them. 'We have to work together so—'

'I know, God, I know,' she interrupted, her gaze beseeching. 'I'm sorry, I just…can't stop thinking about how much I embarrassed myself on Wednesday night, and you said it wouldn't be weird or awkward, but it is. It really, really is. And that's on me, and I'm just so sorry.'

Aaron shook his head, taking a step towards her because he didn't want her feeling like this, but he didn't know how to convince her. He wanted to grab her arms and squeeze them a little to really get it across but he kept his hands by his sides.

'You *didn't* embarrass yourself. You should try barging into a woman's hotel room in the middle of the night. A woman you don't know and is in nothing but her underwear and you're going to be working with her two days later. *That's* something to be embarrassed about. To be sorry about.'

Her snort was full of derision. '*That* was an accident. *My*…action was deliberate. God.' She shut her eyes briefly and shook her head. When they flashed open again they were full of anguish and she leaned in towards him, as if to implore him. 'You were just being kind and welcoming and I must have come across as the worst kind of sex-starved...' She bugged her eyes at him, leaning in closer. 'Widow. Making a play for the first guy I've been alone with in three years. I totally blew it and I just...' She shook her head. 'I'm so sorry.'

Her impassioned tirade hit Aaron square in the chest, her torment over the incident palpable, and he couldn't take the rawness of it. His heart was beating fast and his breath was as heavy as wet sand in his lungs. She seemed to be under the impression that she'd been the only one feeling something on Wednesday night.

And he just couldn't bear it.

Lifting hands he'd had clenched at his sides, he slid them either side of her face as he swooped in and kissed her—hard—trying to convey that she hadn't been alone in that moment. That her kissing him had not been some kind of unwanted advance.

Her clipboard clattering to the floor broke the spell and Aaron pulled away, his hands dropping to his sides again. For something that hadn't been more than a pressing to-gether of lips, he was breathing rough. So was she.

Bending over, he scooped up the clipboard

then handed it back. She took it and they stared at each other for several long beats, not saying anything.

'You and I are going to have to stop apologising to each other all the time,' he said when he found his voice, although it was rough, gravelly. 'I *liked* it...the kiss on Wednesday night.' His eyes burned into hers. 'You weren't the only one who was feeling it, you know?'

Her eyes searched his for what felt like for ever. She swallowed. 'Okay...'

It sounded tentative, but she wasn't rejecting the premise of his statement, which was a relief. 'But, here's the thing,' Aaron continued, his voice a low murmur. 'I think you're still in love with your husband and, as I said on Wednesday night, I don't get involved with out-of-towners, so what say you and I just be friends? Do you think we can do that?'

'Uh-huh.' Her voice was stronger, surer. 'I'd like to.'

Aaron smiled. 'Me too.' Truth was, he'd like a lot more, but there was no way he could see it ending well for him. Why borrow trouble?

Just then the store room door opened and Chelsea's eyes widened as she looked at him.

'Chelsea?' It was Charmaine. 'Are you still in here?'

'Yes…sorry,' she called, her eyes never leaving Aaron's. 'Just finished. I'm coming now.' She started to back away, shoving her pen back through her hair, and Aaron gave her his friendliest smile because, man…that move would be the death of him, he just knew it.

Finally, breaking eye contact, she turned away from him and Aaron's gaze snagged on the swish of her pony tail and the poke of her pen as she turned right at the end and disappeared from sight.

The door closed and Aaron let out a long, slow breath, confident that Chelsea and him were on the same page with the *friends* thing. And it didn't matter how much that kiss—or the one on Wednesday night—had affected him. Had made him want *things*. They were on track to managing the situation between them so he just wasn't going to think about inconvenient truths. Or those kisses.

Yeah… He was never going to think about *them* again.

CHAPTER FOUR

By the time Chelsea's beeper went off the following Thursday evening, she was mentally ready to go out with Aaron in the plane for the first time on an emergency retrieval to an Outback property. She'd had enough short bouts of exposure to him the past week to feel confident about their interactions, and the idea of accompanying him into the middle of nowhere to an accidental gunshot wound to a femoral artery didn't fill her with panic.

He'd suggested they be friends and, as the excruciating embarrassment of her bungled kiss had ebbed in the face of their growing familiarity, interacting with him had begun to feel more natural. Maybe there'd never be that level of easy banter she already shared with the rest of the team but she'd challenge any outsider to say their exchanges weren't friendly.

Buckling up in the King Air, the stretcher

immediately in front of her, a familiar buzz hummed through Chelsea's veins. She'd been in the air three times already this week, flying with Julie and Trent to community clinics in the region. They'd been fun and interesting, and she'd learned so much about how things were done within the organisation and the expectations of the people they served, but this was to her first emergency situation and her pulse kicked up.

That could, of course, have something to do with Aaron buckling up diagonally opposite, his chair facing hers, but she refused to give that thought any air time.

'You guys ready for take-off?' Hattie asked via the cushioned headphone set already snug around Chelsea's ears and doing a very good job of blocking out the propellor noise.

'Roger that,' Aaron confirmed into the mic sitting close to his mouth on the end of the angled arm that protruded from the left cup of his earphones. His voice, deep and confident, sounded simultaneously close yet far away. He smiled at Chelsea and shot her the thumbs-up.

'Roger,' Chelsea also confirmed into her mic as she returned the thumbs-up.

The plane started to taxi to the airstrip and

Chelsea turned her head, looking out of the window, watching the OA hangar get smaller in the fading light. She ran through what they knew about their patient, who was situated four hundred kilometres north-west on an isolated property. He was a twenty-two-year-old man who'd been out kangaroo-shooting with his mates. Quite how he'd come to be shot in the leg was vague, the more pertinent fact being that, by the time they arrived in forty-five minutes, the wound would be two hours old.

Of course, it was still way faster than it would have been for the patient to get to a hospital. A lot could go wrong in two hours where blood loss was involved, and the young guy had apparently bled a lot initially until someone had thought to apply a tourniquet using a belt. The bleeding had reportedly slowed dramatically, but if a large vessel had been compromised in his thigh then blood loss could be significant. The guy involved already had an elevated pulse and was clammy to the touch.

Having a tourniquet on for a long period of time was not ideal either. It could be lifesaving in the face of catastrophic bleeding, but it could also compromise circulation to the entire limb, and cause a build-up of toxins which could have a detrimental effect when it was eventually released.

His friends had loaded him on the back of a ute and had driven him to the airstrip. Most large properties in the Outback had an airstrip for things like deliveries of supplies and mail, and of course for emergencies, and Hattie had been given the co-ordinates. The strip was dirt, and had apparently been graded last month, but the guys on the ground had been instructed to inspect the surface, make sure it was clear of any debris and check for any kangaroos in the vicinity.

They were also going to place lit kerosene lamps from the shed situated off to the side of the parking apron, ninety metres apart down either side of the strip. Compared to what Chelsea was used to in the UK, it all seemed a bit like the Wild West. Farms didn't have their own airstrips and no one had ever been instructed to check for kangaroos—but it added to the adrenaline.

A few minutes later, they lifted into the dying golden light of evening, the sky streaked with gilded clouds. The ground, the hangar and the lights of Balanora quickly fell away as the King Air climbed towards the first stars just blinking through the veil of night.

'ETA forty minutes,' Hattie's voice informed them as the plane levelled out shortly after.

'Roger,' Aaron murmured into his mic. Glancing over at her, he fiddled with the dial on the right ear cup of the headset, obviously changing channels to a private one for just the two of them. 'You ready for this?' he asked. His words, his voice, flowed directly into her ear, causing a tiny shiver.

She nodded. 'Pumped.'

'Might be a bit of a bumpy landing.'

Chelsea shrugged. She'd been landing on dirt strips all week. 'I think I'm getting used to it.'

'Trust me, this will be worse,' he said with a laugh. 'The strips at the communities where you've been the last few days are well-used and well-maintained. A lot of the remote strips on properties are pretty rough and ready.'

It was odd for him to be so close, his mouth moving, his eyes fixed on hers, and yet for him to sound so far away, as if he were in the middle of a vacuum. She was used to the phenomenon but it always felt a little disjointed.

'Hattie doesn't seem too concerned.'

He chuckled. 'Hattie could land one of

these blindfolded in the middle of a dust storm on a dry creek bed with one hand tied behind her back.'

His laughter unfurled delicious tendrils through her body, and the shiver became a trail of goose bumps along the top of her scalp and across her nape. 'Good to know,' she said with a grin, ignoring the goose bumps and the unfurling.

'Don't worry,' he assured her, his gaze earnest. 'She'll get us down safely. And, if she thinks it's not safe, she just won't land. It's always safety first. She won't risk any of our lives or damaging a precious, expensive resource such as this plane.'

Chelsea nodded. She knew that pilots always put the safety of people on board and that of the aircraft first but it was still comforting to have that reiterated. Comforting too that Aaron knew Hattie so well, and there was an obvious bond of trust between them that came from years of flying together. During her time in the UK Chelsea had got to know a few of the chopper pilots she'd flown with, but there were so many of them in a busy twenty-four-hour city medivac hub, it was rare to go up more than two or three times with the same pilot.

It was another thing she was looking forward to—getting to know the team the way Aaron did. Becoming part of this well-oiled machine she'd witnessed all week.

Aaron switched them back to the combined channel and turned his attention to the paperwork he had on his lap. Chelsea gazed out of the window, darkness encroaching on the vast red swathes of earth broken occasionally by narrow veins of green that followed river banks, or the more circular patterns of grass formed around the edges of a dam or billabong.

She watched until the day had completely leached from the landscape and nothing more could be seen apart from an occasional light or small cluster of lights on the ground.

With Aaron still busy, she switched on her overhead light and pulled her current read— a saga set in Sydney—out of her bag. Occasional chatter in her earphones between Hattie and comms broke the cushioned silence created by the noise-cancelling ability of her earphones, but it didn't rouse Chelsea from the story until Hattie announced some time later, 'There she blows.'

Chelsea glanced out the window as Aaron capped his pen. Down below, two straight lines of lights lit up the runway.

'Comms have confirmation from the guys

on the ground that the strip is safe to land,' Hattie said.

Aaron, who had pushed the angled mouthpiece up and away from his mouth earlier, pulled it down again. 'Thanks, Hattie. Comms, any update on the patient condition?'

'No worse. Patient's pain level, eight out of ten, GCS fifteen,' a male voice informed them.

'Roger that. Thank you.' The plane banked to the left as Aaron looked across at her. 'You got all that?'

Chelsea nodded. 'Yes.'

'We should be on the ground in a couple of minutes,' he said.

She shot him the thumbs-up as a tiny hit of adrenaline sparked at her middle. Nerves over not being fully familiar with the plane and where things were kept tap danced in her belly, but Aaron had assured her earlier that the job should be a scoop and run, so they shouldn't need anything too complicated. Getting the patient back to Balanora and hospital for surgical intervention ASAP was their priority.

Chelsea's ears popped as the plane descended. 'Okay,' Hattie said, her voice steely,

'Going in to land. Hold tight you two, might be a bit bumpy.'

Keeping her eyes on the window, Chelsea saw the first few ground lights flash by then the wheels touched down with a jolt and she braced her feet on the floor as she was jostled about. Glancing over at Aaron, she found him braced too, but grinning, and he let out a loud, *'Whoop!'* She laughed.

'You're a legend, Hattie,' he said into his mouthpiece.

'I know,' Hattie replied, and they both laughed.

Within two minutes the plane had taxied into the parking apron and Chelsea unbuckled herself when it pulled to a halt. So did Aaron. The engines cut out and they both took off their headphones simultaneously. 'How was your first Outback property landing?' he asked.

'Amazing!' Because it had been, and she was totally pumped to get out there.

It took another minute for the props to come to a full halt, during which they both donned gloves. As soon as Hattie opened the door, it was action stations. Chelsea exited the plane first into the warmth of the night, a large bag full of supplies slung over her shoulder and Aaron hot on her heels.

The ute was being parked about three metres away towards the rear of the plane as her feet hit the ground. Their patient was on the back tray along with two other guys, and two more sprang from the ute as soon as the engine cut out, pointing torches at Chelsea and Aaron's feet to light the way.

'Hi,' she said as she approached, the fluorescent letters of her shirt reflecting brightly. 'I'm Chelsea.' She smiled at the faces both on and around the ute, harried expressions telling more than words what they'd been through. 'And who do we have here?'

'You hear that, Gazza?' one of the guys joked. 'They sent the bloody Queen of England herself to rescue you.'

Chelsea laughed, as did the patient, albeit it somewhat weak. 'Lucky me.'

'Hey, Brando,' Aaron said. 'I always knew you'd shoot someone with that bloody gun one day.'

'Aaron, man,' the guy called Brando said. 'Sure glad to see you.' He sounded it too. Every one of the grimy, night-shrouded faces was looking at them as if they were the cavalry.

'All good.' Aaron nodded. 'We'll take over from here.'

And take over they did, two guys helping

Chelsea up onto the tray, then moving out of her way while Aaron sprang up unaided like a freaking gazelle, as if he'd been leaping on and jumping off ute trays his entire life.

'Hey, Gazza,' Chelsea said as she got her first look at the patient's face, the torch beams flooding the area. 'How are you feeling?'

He shut his eyes against the light. 'I've had better days.'

It was encouraging to hear him able to joke, but there was a definite pallor to his skin, and his arm was cool to touch despite the heavy coat that had been placed over his torso.

'You kept him warm, that's good,' Chelsea murmured to the guys as she reached for the new oxygen mask she'd hooked up to a cylinder in the emergency bag before they'd taken off. Keeping a shocked patient warm was basic first aid.

'Derek said we should do that,' one of them said.

'Absolutely, you did everything right,' she assured him as she applied the mask to Gazza's face and turned the oxygen up high. All the guys had blood stains on their clothes, so it had obviously been a team effort. 'You put on a tourniquet, you kept him warm, you got help. You did good.'

All the while she talked, Chelsea worked by the torch light, putting on a finger probe to measure oxygen saturation, applying a blood-pressure cuff and slapping electrical dots on Gazza's chest so they could monitor his heart rhythm. The portable monitor bleeped to life with a green squiggle that indicated a normal rhythm but was definitely too fast at a hundred and twenty beats.

Aaron worked too, doing a quick inspection of the wound. The fabric of Gazza's jeans had already been cut away, exposing the location of the injury a few inches above the knee. A cloth soaked in dark red was covering the site and around it another cloth—a T-shirt, maybe, given one of the guys was shirtless—had been tied to secure the make-shift dressing. It was bloodied too but not soaked, which was encouraging. Chelsea knew Aaron wouldn't remove it, wouldn't risk disturbing whatever haemostasis had been achieved.

'Looks like blood loss has been staunched,' Aaron said as he inspected the belt that sat several inches above the entry wound. He wouldn't remove it either.

'BP one hundred systolic,' Chelsea said. Not too bad, considering.

'Okay.' Aaron nodded. 'Let's get in two large bore IVs.'

Under the torchlight, and with Chelsea assisting, both were placed in the large veins in the crook of each elbow within five minutes. She used Brando and Waz, the other guy in the back of the ute, as IV poles, tasking them with holding up the bags of IV fluids.

'Let's run them wide open,' Aaron said.

Chelsea didn't need the instruction, already opening the clamp all the way on her side as Aaron did the same on his. Hopefully the replacement fluid would rally Gazza's system until he could get a transfusion.

'Could someone please take off his right shoe?' Chelsea asked as she plucked the pen from her ponytail and noted his obs in a quick scribble on the glove she was wearing.

The boot was off quick-smart and Aaron sprang off the ute to feel for foot pulses. 'Nothing,' he said when Chelsea raised an eyebrow at him several beats later.

'Okay.'

She made a note of that and the time on her glove as Aaron said, 'He's ready to go. I'll grab the stretcher.' And he strode towards the King Air.

'Is that bad?' the guy who took the boot off asked.

Chelsea smiled at him. 'It means the tourniquet has been very effective.'

She wasn't about to reel off all the potentially damaging side effects of applying a tourniquet for long periods of time and how controversial tourniquets in first aid were, going in and out of fashion over the years, and the plethora of conflicting advice about duration. The bottom line was, without it Gazza would probably be dead. They could do something about any potential circulation compromise when he got to hospital.

Nothing could be done about death.

'Okay, guys.' Aaron approached with the stretcher. 'We're going to need your help to get Gazza loaded.'

'Where do you need us?' Brando said.

CHAPTER FIVE

Two hours later, they were back in Balanora. Gazza had been taken away by the ambulance and was currently undergoing an emergency operation performed by the visiting flying surgeon to stabilise him enough for aerial transfer to Brisbane for further treatment and management. Hattie had gone home half an hour ago and Chelsea had just finished restocking the plane.

It had been Aaron's turn but Chelsea had wanted to do it so she could keep familiarising herself with where things were, both in the store room and on board. Once she was done, she bade Brett, who was doing checks on the King Air, a goodnight before making her way to the office to find Aaron.

'Hey,' he said, looking up from the keyboard as she opened the door.

The main office was usually brightly lit but

at this hour the only light on was the one directly above the desk Aaron occupied.

'Hi.'

It was the first time they'd been alone together at work since the store room and she felt weirdly shy. But it *was* ten o'clock, and kind of dark, with a hush that was the complete opposite of the daytime bustle.

It made her very aware of him, of her attraction to him.

'How do you think it went tonight?' Aaron asked, leaning casually back in his chair.

Chelsea forced her legs to move closer until she was on the other side of his desk. 'I think it went well.' Unless…he didn't think so? 'Why, did I do something wrong?'

'What?' He chuckled. '*No.* You were great. It was just your first emergency call out, so I wanted to check you were okay with how everything went. Ask if you had any questions or observations.'

'Oh.' Chelsea shot him a rueful smile. 'Right. I think it all went smoothly and that Gazza was lucky to have mates who kept their cool. You know them?'

'Not really. Just Brando. I played footy with a couple of his brothers.'

She nodded. 'You think the tourniquet being on for that long will affect the viability of his leg?' His foot had been alarmingly cold and dusky during the flight.

He shrugged. 'It could do. It'll have probably been on for about four hours by the time they take it off. There wasn't another choice, though.'

'Yeah.' Truer words had never been spoken. It had been the ultimate 'rock and a hard place' scenario. 'It'll be interesting to know how he fares.'

'Charmaine will follow up over the coming days and let us know.'

'Excellent.' In her previous jobs there'd been *so* many incidents attended, it had sometimes been hard to keep track. But Chelsea guessed it was different in such a small, tight-knit community.

'Question.' Aaron sat forward in his chair and sifted through some paperwork. Finding what he was looking for, he handed it across to her, pointing with his pen at a numeral. 'Is this a four or a seven? It looks like a seven but that would be odd.'

Chelsea leaned in, taking the patient observation chart from him and inspecting the notation she'd made on the plane. 'It's a four,' she confirmed, passing it back.

His eyebrows drew together as he looked at

it again. 'Note to self,' he murmured. 'Chelsea's fours look like sevens.'

She laughed. 'No way. That is clearly a four.'

Letting the piece of paper slide from his fingers, he shook his head. 'And they say doctors have terrible hand writing.'

'They do,' Chelsea said. Except Aaron's, of course, which, despite its bold strokes and slashes, was entirely legible. 'Yours is an exception.'

'What's that you say?' He put a hand to his ear as if he was trying to hear better. 'I'm exceptional?'

He grinned and Chelsea's breath caught in her throat. An outsider might have concluded that he was flirting but, after a week of observing the team and him working together, she knew this was just Aaron being Aaron, bantering as he would with anyone else on the team.

Which was a good thing.

Due to their rocky start, they hadn't got into that groove yet, so maybe this was his attempt to get there. Chelsea was more than willing to pick up what he was putting down because, as soon as their friendship felt more natural, the better for everyone.

'Ha! Good try. Not quite the same thing there, buddy.'

An expression of surprise flickered over his face—whether at her returning his banter or her use of the word 'buddy', she didn't know—but it was gone as quickly as it came as he clutched at his chest. 'Careful, you'll dent my giant doctor ego.'

Her first instinct was to deny he had any such thing. She had worked with some super egos in her past and Aaron's didn't come close. But she went for banter instead. 'Then my work here is done.'

He chuckled and, yes, Chelsea *did* feel the deep resonance of it brushing seductively against her skin. But, hey, Rome wasn't built in a day, right? 'You done with restocking?' he asked.

Grateful for the subject change, Chelsea grabbed it with both hands. 'Yep. All ready for the next take-off.'

'Good-oh.' He nodded. 'You might as well go, then.'

Chelsea shook her head. 'What about you?'

'No, no.' He sighed dramatically. 'I'll be here for hours yet deciphering your writing, but you go on home and get your beauty sleep.'

'Hey,' she protested with a laugh, even though she could see by the twinkle in those grey eyes he was joking. 'Serve yourself right if you are,' she quipped.

Okay, this was *good*. This was feeling really good now. Friends. Banter. *Natural*.

He grinned. 'I'll see you tomorrow.'

'Unless I see you tonight.' An awkward moment passed between them and Chelsea hastened to clarify. 'You know…if we get called out again.'

'Yeah.' He smiled. 'I know.'

'Right, then.' She tapped the desk. 'Good-night.'

'Night.'

She was halfway to the door when he called her name and she turned to find him looking at her, the spill of light overhead bathing his hair in a golden aura. Something tugged hard down deep and low.

'You did good out there.'

Chelsea didn't need his praise. She knew she'd done a good job because she was confident in her experience and ability, no matter how new and unfamiliar the environment. But she *liked* it nonetheless.

'Thank you,' she said, before turning and continuing on her way.

Sunday afternoon, Chelsea found herself knocking on Trent's door. He'd called that

morning to invite her to an impromptu barbecue in her honour—a get-to-know-the-new-
girl thing. Stupidly, she'd assumed it was just
going to be Trent and his wife, Siobhan, but
when she arrived a fashionable fifteen minutes late, with the requested folding chair and
a bottle of wine to share, a party was in full
swing.

Music met them as Trent ushered her into
a back yard playing host to clusters of laughing, chatting people. Some she recognised
from work—hell, she'd recognised Aaron
immediately, her eyes drawn to him and a
pretty blonde in a midriff top—but a lot she
didn't know.

'Oh.' She pulled up short. 'You haven't
gone to all this trouble for me, I hope?'

'Of course,' he said cheerily, slinging an
arm around her shoulder and giving her
upper arm a brisk squeeze. 'You're the guest
of honour and we're welcoming you, Balanora style. Suck it up, sweetheart.'

'Trent Connor.' A tall, curvy redhead with
an Irish accent approached. 'I told you not to
spring it on her,' she chastised, but the lilt in
her accent softened it dramatically. She shook
her head at Chelsea. 'What's he like?' She
stuck out her hand. 'I'm Siobhan.'

'It's lovely to meet you, Siobhan,' Chelsea said absently as they shook hands.

'Come on, then.' Siobhan took the chair and the wine off Chelsea and passed them to Trent. 'I'm going to introduce Chelsea around to some people. Be a darling and get her some of that to drink. She looks like she can do with it.'

'Yes, my little Irish clover,' Trent said with an adoring smile.

Chelsea was whisked away then, meeting person after person until her head spun. There were partners and children of OA staff she'd already met and those she hadn't. Also, several more doctors and nursing staff from the Balanora hospital. There were teaching colleagues of Siobhan's from the primary school, as well as about a dozen young local professionals working for places such as the council, the railway, Department of Parks and Wildlife, estate agents, tourism bodies and various other businesses around town.

It seemed Trent and Siobhan knew everyone and, despite the surprise nature of the party, Chelsea enjoyed herself immensely. Between meeting so many new people and getting to know Siobhan—who was an absolute hoot—the very pleasant afternoon under the shady backyard gums flew into early evening.

She even spoke to Aaron for a while who, unlike every other man at the party, was drinking some kind of fizzy juice instead of something alcoholic because he was on call until seven the next morning. He introduced her to the woman she'd seen him with when she'd first arrived, who turned out to be Gazza's sister, Maddie.

It was great to catch up on his progress, and Chelsea was relieved to find out that the leg hadn't suffered any detrimental effects from the tourniquet, and that the doctors in Brisbane were already talking about a discharge date some time in the next few days.

'Dinner's up!' Trent yelled just after six, rallying everyone to the barbecue area to grab something to eat.

Chelsea's stomach growled as the delicious aromas of cooking food saw her join the mass migration to the undercover patio. She hadn't realised she was so hungry until now. While in the queue for her food, she and Siobhan swapped stories of life back home.

'How'd you end up here?' Chelsea asked.

'The same as most people. Came out on a backpacking holiday a decade ago, met Trent at the Crown and been here ever since.'

Laughing at the matter-of-factness of Siobhan's statement, Chelsea said, 'Have you been back to Ireland at all?'

'Couple of times. Introduced Trent to the family. Showed him around the country. But this land…it owns him.' She shrugged. 'And I don't want to be anywhere he's not.'

'How have you found the heat?'

Siobhan laughed. 'Not my favourite part of the Outback,' she admitted. 'But I acclimatised pretty quickly. And frankly I'd prefer it to the bloody flies.'

Having experienced those flies already, Chelsea was beginning to understand the common refrain. She'd not uttered it yet but she was in no doubt that she would.

'Okay, what'll it be?' Trent asked as they reached the start of the queue. 'I have chicken pieces, rib fillet and kangaroo snags.'

Chelsea blinked. 'Really?' Although curious, Chelsea had no desire to try the meat from such an iconic Australian animal. Where she harked from, kangaroos were considered cute—not a culinary delicacy.

He tossed his head back and laughed. 'No.'

'Ignore him.' Siobhan rolled her eyes affectionately. 'They're beef and pork. Although, kangaroo meat is highly nutritious and less than two percent fat.'

'Noted,' Chelsea said to Siobhan before turning back to Trent. 'I'll have some chicken, please.'

After she'd eaten, an impromptu touch football game between the teachers sprang up. There was much laughter and friendly sledging from the sidelines, and when it came to an end Chelsea was roped into a game, despite insisting, as Trent grabbed her hand, that she'd never played before.

'Come on, medical staff,' Trent called. 'Let's go.'

'Hospital versus the OA,' Charmaine suggested as she joined the people forming up in the middle of the back yard.

Trent shook his head. 'Doctors versus nurses.'

'That gives you three local A-grade footy players on your team,' she pointed out. Apparently two of the nurses from the hospital played in the local competition too.

'You have Aaron,' Trent returned.

The man in question dropped his head to either side to stretch his traps as he gripped a foot behind him and stretched out a quad muscle. His shorts, already mid-thigh, rode up, and Chelsea couldn't help but notice it was a *very nice* quad muscle. 'I can take 'em all, don't worry, Charmaine.'

'Plus,' Trent added, 'We have Chelsea, who's never played before and probably doesn't even know the rules. That's like a handicap.'

'Hey,' Chelsea said with a laugh. 'I thought I was the guest of honour.'

'Sorry, Chels,' Trent said, not sounding remotely sorry. 'Guest time's over! This is footy.'

'Yeah, *Chels*,' Aaron teased, a crooked smile hovering on that crooked mouth. 'Footy's serious business around here.'

She wasn't sure she was a fan of having her name shortened but, given it seemed to be a way to express affection out here, a trill of pleasure bubbled up from her middle. Maybe it was a sign that she was becoming one of the gang.

She nodded good-naturedly but stuck her hands on her hips, her feet firmly apart in a Wonder Woman pose as she shot Aaron a *faux* steely look. 'Looks like I better bring my A-game, huh?'

There were a few 'Ooh's from the crowd as Aaron laughed. 'You better bring your A-plus,' he said, matching her stance and tone, 'Because doctors demolish.'

The half-dozen people behind him cheered,

'Doctors demolish!', smashing their fists in the air.

Trent laughed. 'Whatever gets you through the night, big guy. Everyone knows nurses annihilate.'

'Oh, Jaysus,' Siobhan said from the make-shift sideline that had been outlined with white plates. 'You two going to play or should I just get out me ruler so you can measure your dicks?'

Everyone laughed and the game got underway. It took all of a minute for Chelsea to be glad she'd put on shorts and not the strappy sundress she'd almost worn, lest it would have ended up over her head from the physicality of the game. It might only be touch football but there were plenty of spills as members of each team smack-talked back and forth.

Aaron had been right—footy was serious business!

'Hey, ref!' Aaron called, pointing at Trent ten minutes into the second half. 'Offside.'

Siobhan had taken on the role of referee. 'Yeah, yeah.' She rolled her eyes at Chelsea who was standing nearby. 'Anybody'd think they were playing for bloody sheep stations.'

Chelsea grinned and used the back of her forearm to dash at some sweat as Siobhan awarded a penalty to the nurses. The play started again and this time, by some kind of miracle, Chelsea managed to intercept the ball for the first time. She stared at it in her hands for a nanosecond before everyone roared, *'Run!'* and she took off for the try line.

The closest member of the opposition team to her was Aaron—in fact he was suddenly very close indeed, his presence big as he loped just behind and to her left. Chelsea's heartbeat kicked up in a way that didn't have much to do with the exertion and more to do with having Aaron hot on her heels. The anticipation of feeling the tips of his fingers landing in the small of her back, of him *touching* her in front of everyone, no matter how impersonally, caused her to shiver despite how damn hot she was.

She knew there was no way she could outrun him—he was too muscular, too pumped, for that—but she was smaller and nimbler, a fact she proved when he reached for her and said, 'Gotcha, *Chels.*'

Except he hadn't. Her last-second dodge managed to evade his touch. 'Think again, Azza,' she taunted, the cheers of everyone around her filling the night air and her head as she strode for the line which seemed as if it was getting further and further away.

His warm chuckle, so close, followed her and she knew there was no way Aaron would make the same mistake again. So, with the line approaching, she made a dive for it, looking over her shoulder in what felt like slow motion as he too dove, his outstretched fingers coming closer and closer.

She turned back just in time to brace for impact, the ball touching the ground before his hand touched her back. Laughing at her triumph, she performed a quick roll to twist out of Aaron's path but he countered, his reactions quicker than the processing of the information that the ball had already been grounded, his body landing sprawled on top of her, his torso half-pressing her into the grass, one meaty thigh tangling between hers.

Somewhere Siobhan yelled, *'Try!'* and her team mates hollered as they all ran towards her. But Chelsea was oblivious. She was only slightly winded by the impact but the effects of Aaron—big and strong, pinning her to the ground with his body—were far more cataclysmic.

They were both laughing, but not for long. Hers died pretty quickly as the thrust of the thigh she had admired earlier pressed between her legs. His followed not long after, as if he too was just realising their position. His gaze zeroed in on her mouth as a hot, dark look passed between them.

They might have agreed to be friends, but Chelsea had no doubt that, had they been alone, they'd be doing more than staring at each other right now, wondering who was going to make the first move. One of them would already have made it.

But they weren't alone and suddenly Trent was there, grabbing Aaron by the shoulder. 'C'mon, get off her, you great big lug, we need to congratulate our girl.'

Whether he was dragged off or rolled off, Chelsea wasn't sure. All she knew was she was suddenly being pulled up and enveloped in the centre of a huge team hug, a lump the size of London lodging in her throat. Grief had seen her withdraw from her social life three years ago. The complicated feelings she'd been experiencing since finding out about Dom hadn't loaned themselves to her being particularly social.

She'd missed it, she realised—just hanging out with colleagues. With...*friends.*

The fact that all these people in this tiny

town were now in her friend circle made the moment even more bitter sweet.

'Okay, okay,' Trent said after a bit. 'We still got a few minutes of this half! Let's go kick some more arse.'

The huddle broke up and Chelsea realised Aaron was still lying on the ground on his back. She wondered briefly if he'd been hurt until their gazes locked and the same flare of heat she'd felt when she'd been under him only moments ago burned between them again.

Trent broke the connection by bouncing the football off Aaron's forehead, who swore at him. 'Get up, old man.' Trent grinned. 'We're winning.'

Just then the two beepers Siobhan had been holding—one for Aaron, one for Renee—went off. Everyone around paused as Aaron performed a perfect sit-up, and Siobhan handed both beepers over to their respective owners.

'Car accident.' Aaron read off the screen. 'Two hundred clicks south of town.' Rising from the ground in one smooth move that did funny things to Chelsea's insides, he glanced at Trent. 'Rain check, dude.'

'Any time.' They fist-bumped then Trent

clapped his hands. 'Okay, who's going to sub in for hotshot here?'

Someone—a cousin of Trent's whom Chelsea thought was a dentist—stepped forward but she only really had eyes for Aaron as their gazes met and lingered one last time before he said to Renee, 'Meet you at the base in twenty?' and they departed together.

Aaron worked hard the following week to act normally around Chelsea after their crash-tackle incident—no easy feat. He knew he hadn't been alone in that heightened moment and that, had no one been around, it would have had a very different outcome. And every time their gazes had met this week he'd seen that same recognition in her eyes too, no matter how fleeting.

Still, despite the counsel of his wiser angels whispering about the friend zone, his attraction hadn't lessened. Unfortunately, his brain and his body were just not on the same page. The fact that he really *liked* her didn't help. These past couple of weeks, she'd fitted in seamlessly with the team—quick with a laugh, a joke or whip-smart comeback and good-natured about all the teasing over her accent, not to mention efficient, methodical and *kind*.

Everyone—without exception, it seemed—had taken to OA's newest member of staff.

In a lot of ways, liking her was worse than lusting after her, because the latter he could dismiss as bodily urges and that kept him vigilant about maintaining distance. The former made him want to draw closer. To really get to know her and deepen the friendship he'd insisted they have. But he was hyper-aware that the line between the two states was razor-thin and deepening one would inevitably ramp up the other.

And it had only been a couple of weeks!

Thankfully, albeit coincidentally, they hadn't worked together this week, which helped. Not on any of the clinic runs or the three emergency retrievals. They hadn't even been on call together. It wouldn't always be that way, he knew, but perhaps until he was used to being around her, used to this crazy kind of tug he felt whenever she was near, just exchanging a few brief words here and there as they passed by was enough.

Except the universe, it seemed, was determined to keep pushing them together. He took a phone call from Meg on Friday, the first day of his rostered three days off, asking him if he could pick up and deliver a book case to Chelsea's. Dan, her partner, had been tasked with doing it but had been called out of town for work for the day.

'I'm sure it could wait till tomorrow,' Meg said, 'But I know you have the day off, and Chels was so excited last night about finally getting her books unpacked.'

Yes, *Chels* had stuck.

Ordinarily, Aaron would have been keen to help out in this kind of situation, particularly for a new member of their team. He had the vehicle and the brawn, after all, and had already previously offered. But she'd gone to Dan for assistance with the bookshelf—not him—which told Aaron all he needed to know about how much she wanted to avoid being alone with him.

Something he utterly endorsed.

But now Meg had asked him to do it and it would seem odd for him to refuse when she not only knew he was free, but that Aaron would have done it for any other staff member without thinking twice. Sure, he was going to Curran Downs today, but hadn't planned to leave until after lunch, which Meg also knew.

And then there was the way Chelsea's voice had softened when she'd spoken about her books, as if they were her friends…

So, here he was, knocking on her door at

nine in the morning after picking the flat-packed boxes up from a house in the older part of town. Chelsea had obviously taken his advice about the thriving local buy-sell-swap site and found two brand-new book-cases, still in their boxes.

He propped the first box against the bricks beside the door and didn't wait for an answer before turning back for the remaining box. The door opened just as he was lifting it out of the tray of the ute.

'Oh. You're…not Dan,' Chelsea said, sounding discombobulated by his presence.

She could join the club, because that short dress brushing her legs at mid-thigh and her bare feet were utterly discombobulating him. Her was hair was piled up in that messy up-do again, several silken strands falling around her nape.

'He got called out of town for work this morning,' Aaron explained as he carried the box towards her. 'Meg rang and asked me to do it.'

'Okay, well…thank you.' She smiled. 'I appreciate it.'

'It's what we do around here,' he said dis-missively. 'Help each other out.'

Which was the truth, but he realised he probably sounded curt rather than neighbourly, and he ground his teeth at his ineptitude. *What the hell, dude?*

He leaned the second box on top of the first, the sun on his shoulders already carrying a real bite. But that wasn't what was making him feel hot as he stood two feet from Chelsea—far closer than was good for him. It was the silky slide of her hair, that hint of cleavage at the V of her neckline and her bright-purple toenails that matched the tiny purple flowers of her dress. He had no idea why *toes* were turning him on.

It wasn't as though he had a foot fetish. Or he hadn't had, anyway.

'Could I squeeze past?' he asked. Not that he wanted to *squeeze* at all. He'd prefer she give him a very wide berth.

'Oh, right yes…here. I'll hold the door.'

As if the universe had heard his preference for distance, Chelsea pushed on the screen door, stepping outside to hold it open, giving him plenty of room to pick up both boxes and transport them inside to the blissful oasis of cool. Propping them against the inside wall, he took the first one in to the living room as Chelsea shut the screen and wooden door behind her.

They passed each other as he headed back to get the second box and she looked fresh as a freaking daisy with those flowers swinging around her thighs. She shot him a small smile and Aaron's fingers itched to slide up her arms to her neck, push into her hair and tilt her chin so he could kiss the hell out of her mouth.

Instead, he said, 'You know your electricity bill is going to be a shocker?' Because apparently he was determined to be Stick Up His Butt Guy today.

Either oblivious to his mood, or choosing to ignore it, Chelsea laughed as she crossed to where he'd put the first flat-pack on the floor near the boxes of books. 'Yeah. I do.' She crouched to inspect the pictures on the front. 'It makes me cringe thinking about my footprint every time I flick it on but…*ugh*… hopefully I'll be more acclimatised for next summer.'

Aaron's step faltered at her talk of next year, as though she might actually still be around, but he refused to give it, or the flare of hope it caused, any oxygen. A year was a long time in the dust, the heat and the flies for someone not used to any of it.

'Everyone acclimatises at a different rate,' he said noncommittally as he placed the second flat-pack on top of the first.

Some never did at all.

Even twenty years after leaving, his mother still recalled the heat of the Outback with a visible shudder.

Despite the sweat drying rapidly in the cool, a trickle ran from his hair down his temple and he wiped at it with the back of his forearm. 'Oh, God,' Chelsea said as she glanced up, catching the action. 'Sorry, you've been carrying heavy loads for me and it's roasting out there.'

'It's fine.'

'Nuh-uh.' She stood. 'Let me get you a cold drink.' Her arm lightly brushed his as she passed and he swore he heard her breath hitch before she continued on her way to the kitchen. 'I have water. Cold or tap. I also have juice if you'd prefer.'

Every instinct Aaron possessed told him to decline the drink and leave. *Just leave, dude.* But it didn't feel right, going without offering to put the flat pack together, and in the end ingrained good manners won out.

'Cold water, please.' Because he *was* thirsty. And, if nothing else, it'd occupy his hands.

'Coming right up.' She turned to the cupboards on the wall opposite to the island bench.

Aaron tried—and failed—*not* to notice the swing of her skirt and the way the hem rose as she reached up and grabbed two glasses. Deliberately turning his attention to the flat packs, he crouched beside them, pulling out the box-cutter he'd stashed in the back pocket of his shorts. Just in case.

'Have you got an Allen key?' He had a bunch in the tool box in the back of his ute along with sundry other items that would probably be handy.

'Yeah, I bought a set of eight yesterday from the hardware shop, because the seller said she'd lost the key that came with it.' He heard some clinking as her voice drew nearer. 'But it's okay, I'll be fine. You don't have to stay.' She nudged his shoulder. 'Here.'

Looking round, he took the frosty glass from her fingers, a vision of little purple flowers brushing against pale shapely thighs searing into his brain. 'Thanks,' he muttered before turning back immediately to the flat packs.

Aaron's heart bumped in his chest as he gulped down the water in several quick swallows, the icy cold an antidote to the heat licking through his veins and singeing his lungs.

'Thank you for delivering these,' Chelsea

continued, clearly oblivious to his inner turmoil as she plonked herself cross-legged on the floor on the other side of the boxes, almost directly in front of him. 'But you're off home today, aren't you?'

Chelsea had come into the staff room yesterday when Aaron had been discussing heading to Curran Downs for his three days off. He didn't think she'd been listening as he and Brett had discussed the pros and cons of dogs versus drones in mustering.

'I can take it from here.' She held up her ring of Allen keys. 'Have tools, will construct.'

She spoke a good game but she was looking at them as though she wasn't sure which end she was supposed to use and Aaron couldn't suppress his chuckle, the tension in his gut and his neck easing a touch. 'I don't mean to call your furniture construction abilities into question but…do you know *how* to put together a flat pack?'

'No, but that's only because I've never tried. It can't be any harder than setting up for ECMO in the ICU, or having to resuscitate a patient who's coded mid-flight, surely?'

Aaron couldn't fault her logic—those were complex and highly specialised medical procedures. 'Not harder, no, just a different kind of skill. Also.' He shrugged. 'Less life and death, so there's that.'

She barked out a laugh, her eyes crinkling and her lips parting, her head falling back a little, the fine escaped tendrils of her hair bushing the bare flesh between her shoulder blades. Aaron's heart went *thunk*. Then he joined her because, really, it *was* just a bloody book case, *not* life and death.

'I'm sure I'll be fine. Plus, I've seen this kind of thing being done loads on DIY shows.'

'You're right,' he conceded. 'It's not that hard once you know what you're doing.'

'There you go then. Plus, I have all day to figure it out. I'll just read the instructions thoroughly and take it one step at a time.'

'Ah, yeah…about that.' Aaron pressed his lips together so he wouldn't smile at her 'what now?' expression. 'The woman who lost the Allen key also couldn't find what she'd done with the instructions.'

She huffed out a sigh, her shoulders slumping as a V formed between her brows. 'No wonder it was so cheap.' But her defeat was only fleeting as she straightened her shoulders. 'Okay, well… I'll just… YouTube it.'

'*Or*, I can do it for you and you can be putting your books into your new bookshelf in an hour.'

Aaron wasn't sure why he was being so damned insistent. He told himself he was just being neighbourly, that he'd do the same for anyone. But he didn't think that was the truth. He just…didn't want to leave. Not yet.

'An hour, huh?'

'*About*. Might take me longer.' He shrugged. 'Might take me shorter.'

'Okay.' Chelsea nodded, looking at him assessingly. 'On one condition.'

'Oh, yeah.' He laughed. 'What's that?'

'I don't want you to do it for me. I want you to show me how to do it for myself.'

Aaron tried not to read between the lines of that statement, but he did wonder if Chelsea was so gung-ho to do it herself as a way to prove her independence. Maybe, he—*Dom*—had been the kind of guy who had done everything for Chelsea. Although, she'd mentioned he'd been deployed *a lot*, so that didn't sound practical. Nor did it sound like the highly competent woman he'd got to know these past couple of weeks.

But maybe carving out her independence was the first step in…*moving on*. Like up-sticking and coming to live on the other side of the planet had been. Because Aaron didn't believe that whole 'adventure' bullshit.

His idiotic heart leapt at the idea before his brain squashed the errant thought harder and faster than a bug on a windscreen. She might be inconveniently attracted to him— something that was entirely mutual—but she *was* holding back and, whether that was because she was still in love with her husband or too afraid to risk her heart again, it didn't end well for him.

It was stupid to feel so envious of a dead man, but Aaron realised he did. Not because he and Chelsea had had a life together but because Dom had known her back before the terrible blow she'd been dealt.

When she hadn't needed to run away.

'If you really want to try and figure this out for yourself, I'm happy to get on my way.' He held up his hands in surrender.

Maybe this stupid book-case assembly *was* just what she needed.

'What?' She cocked a disbelieving eyebrow at him but a smile played on her mouth. 'Are you welching on your offer, Azza? You talked me into it and now you're backing out on the deal? You're sorry now you said an hour, aren't you? Afraid you talked yourself up a bit too much?'

Aaron grinned, assailed by an overwhelming urge to lean across and kiss that smile right off her mouth. He resisted, but only barely.

He laughed. 'Time me, *Chels*.'

CHAPTER SIX

'How do you know what goes where?'

Aaron glanced at Chelsea's perplexed face as they stood side by side, looking at all the pieces he'd laid out on the floor so he could see what was what. 'This isn't my first rodeo, you know.'

'It doesn't look enough. Is it enough?'

'Sure.'

'How do you know? All I see are a bunch of differing lengths of plank and a gazillion screws. With no instructions.'

He shrugged. 'I've grown up tinkering with things. All kinds of engines, running repairs on sheds and fences and water troughs and windmills and tanks and dams. It's just… what you do when you're in the middle of nowhere, with not a lot available and not a lot of money for new things or to hire someone to come and fix stuff. You learn to do things

for yourself. To improvise and be resource-
ful—use what you have at hand.'

She nodded, her head turned slightly to
look at him. 'So, you're a…jack of all trades?'

Aaron laughed, glancing at her. 'Something like that.'

She smiled at him then and he smiled back,
and Aaron was aware, once again, how close
they were. For a second, he even let himself imagine he was free to lift one of those
strands of hair off her neck and drop a kiss
in its place. Then he gave himself a mental
slap upside the head.

'Okay. Let's get this show on the road.'

It took an hour and fifteen minutes to assem-
ble the two three-metre *faux* walnut book-
shelves. Chelsea had been a keen apprentice
who'd picked up the ropes quickly, even if
those purple flowers had been distracting
with a capital D. They stood back to admire
their handiwork, which took up almost the
entire back wall space.

'*That* is freaking awesome.' Chelsea nodded at it, clearly satisfied. 'How's that for
team work?'

She held her hand up to him, clearly after
a high five, and Aaron slapped his palm
against hers. It felt buddy-like and platonic.

Something two friends who'd just worked on a project together *would* do on its completion.

But it only made Aaron aware of how far he had to go until it felt *natural*.

'Not bad at all,' he confirmed.

She laughed. 'See? Shearing sheds and flatpacks—I'm totally kicking adventure arse.'

'Lady…' Aaron shook his head. 'Your definition of adventure su—'

'Needs work,' she cut in, folding her arms as she sent him a mock-stern look.

'Okay, sure.' It was Aaron's turn to laugh. 'Let's go with that.'

'Plus,' she said, bugging her eyes at him. 'I'm not a lady.'

True. Chelsea's plummy English accent reeked of class but she was no wilting flower. 'You only sound like one,' he said with a tone that sounded distinctly like banter.

'You think I should throw in a "crikey" or two and say things like—' she cleared her throat '—that's not a knife, this is a knife?'

Aaron really laughed then. 'Absolutely not.' She sounded as if she were Afrikaans, Kiwi and *drunk* all rolled into one.

'Laugh all you want, buddy boy,' she said with a grin. 'That's exactly how you sound.'

He shuddered. 'I bloody hope not.'

Her brown eyes shimmered with mirth. 'You *bloody do*,' she said, flattening her vowels and deepening her voice, clearly attempting to mimic him now.

Aaron groaned but then he laughed, and she joined him, and they did that for several long moments, just staring at each other and laughing, and Aaron couldn't remember when he'd last enjoyed himself this much with a woman.

Which was why he should leave.

'Well, anyway,' he said as their laughter settled and their eyes didn't seem to be able to unlock. 'I'll…get this rubbish out of your way and you can start loading up your books.'

'Thanks.' She dragged her eyes off him. 'That'd be great.'

Aaron gathered up all the detritus from the assembly and took it out to his ute before heading back inside to say goodbye, because it would be weird just to leave, even if it might be wiser not to put himself in the path of temptation again.

'Um…' Chelsea held up something as he entered the living room, frowning at him. 'Should this be left over?'

She was sitting on the floor surrounded by little piles of books, one of the six boxes open beside her. They were spread out on top of the bookcase, stacked around her on the floor and placed haphazardly here and there on the different shelves.

Aaron plucked the object out of her fingers. It was a screw. 'There's always some random screw left over.'

She quirked an eyebrow. 'If there'd been instructions would there be one left over?'

He grinned as he handed it back, deciding not to tell her that he probably wouldn't have paid more than cursory attention to the directions anyway. 'Of course. It's like the law of flatpacks.'

'The law, huh?'

'Sure. The unwritten kind.'

'Okay.' She laughed. 'As long as the bookcases aren't going to collapse like a house of cards one day, because there's going to be quite a lot of weight in them when I'm done.'

'So I see.' Aaron eyes moved over the multiple towers of books five or six high. And she'd only opened one box. 'I can't believe you have this many.'

'These aren't all.' She made a dismissive gesture with her hand. 'I have about twenty more back in Hackney.'

Aaron refused to read too much into the fact she hadn't brought all the books she professed to love so much and tried to wrap his head around just how many books Chelsea *did* own. 'Twenty?'

'Uh huh,' she said, as if it was the most natural thing in the world to own what must be *hundreds* of books.

'How'd these books make the cut to join you on your *adventures*?'

She smiled at his deliberate use of the word, and he had to look away unless he smiled too and then they'd be smiling at each other. *Again.* He picked up the nearest one off the top of its pile, one by Georgette Heyer. In fact, the whole stack was Heyer books.

Beside that stack was another consisting of classics in their iconic orange cover, and surrounding her on the floor were several piles of what appeared to romance novels, if the covers were anything to go by.

'These ones are my absolute favourites. They made the cut when I moved into Dom's parents' not long after he died. The other twenty are still in storage at a lock-up with all my other stuff.'

There was a lot in that sentence to unpack. Not least of which was, her life was still in boxes in the UK. Which was why he shouldn't be here, trying to be friends when he was just beginning to realise that might not be enough. Also…she'd moved in with her parents-in-law? 'You moved in with your…?'

'Mother-in-law.' She laughed. 'And my father-in-law. Yes.'

'That's…' He cast around for a word that wouldn't cause offence. After all, what did he know? He'd never had in-laws.

'Nutso?'

Aaron barked out a laugh at her candour. 'Well, no, but…it's not something you see a lot of, right?'

'No. And a lot of people thought it wasn't a good idea. But…' Chelsea shrugged. 'I love his parents, we were all grieving and it made sense to be a comfort to each other.'

Her voice had taken on a plaintive quality as her gaze fixed on a point just over his shoulder. He wanted to ask about her parents—had they comforted her? But it felt too personal and she seemed too far away right now.

'It just…' Her gaze focused back on him. 'Worked.'

Which led to the next question. Maybe that was too personal as well, but she had at least opened this door. 'Did it stop working? Is that why you ended up here?'

Shaking her head slowly, she contemplated

him for long moments, her eyes suddenly unbearably sad. 'No.' Her lips pressed together for a beat. 'It was…time.'

Caught up in the raw emotion in her gaze, Aaron nodded. 'When you know, you know, right?' Like his mother, who had drawn her line in the sand.

'Yeah.'

As if she realised she'd exposed too much of herself, Chelsea dropped her gaze to the book in her hand and Aaron, determined not to pry any further, reach for another too. He glanced at the well-loved illustrated cover of a girl, a pig and a spider weaving a web around the title.

'*Charlotte's Web?*' He opened the book. 'This yours?' A name had been written in faded pencil on the inside cover—*Deborah Tanner.*

Looking up at him again, Chelsea nodded with a wistful expression. 'It belonged to my mother, yeah.'

'This is her?' Aaron's thumb brushed over the pencil. 'Deborah?'

'Debbie.' Her gaze shifted to the book, to the way his thumb caressed the page. 'Her name was Debbie.'

Was. Aaron knew that look. He knew that

tone. The weight of it, the bleakness of it. 'She died?'

'When I was four. Car accident.'

'I'm sorry.'

She roused herself, shaking her head. 'I don't really remember her. But I do remember her reading me this book.' She reached for it and Aaron passed it to her, watching as she opened it in her lap and absently flicked through the pages. 'I re-read it usually once a year. Cry every damn time,' she said, with a tiny self-deprecating laugh.

'It looks well-thumbed.'

'Yeah.' She nodded. 'It was well thumbed when she was reading it to me.'

'She was a reader as well?' Aaron was aware he was prying again and he wasn't sure if she wanted him to or if she was seconds away from shutting him down.

'Oh, yes.' Chelsea nodded but didn't look up from her lap. 'I think that's where I got it from.'

'Did your dad take over? After?'

She stared at the book for a long time before shaking her head. 'No. Dad...' She glanced up at him. 'My father...checked out for a lot of years after she died.'

Aaron tried to read between the lines of her carefully chosen words. 'He...gave you up?'

'No.' The loose tendrils of her hair swished against her neck as she shook her head. 'I mean, he provided for me. He went to work, earned a living. I had all the things I needed for school and hobbies and university. I wasn't...neglected.'

'Physically.' But *emotionally*...?

'Yeah.' She nodded as if in acknowledgement of what he *hadn't* said. 'That was all he was capable of, really. His grief was... all-consuming. It was enough for him to just put one foot in front of the other most days, you know?'

Aaron nodded. 'Yeah. I know.' His mother hadn't died but they had lost her nonetheless, and his father had certainly grieved in the only way men of his generation from land knew how to do—stoically. Ironically, he and his sister had the drought to thank for holding their father back from a much darker state, with the station and the sheep demanding every last skerrick of his attention.

It could have been very different.

'Having me there probably kept him back from the abyss but I was also an...intrusion in a lot of ways. Which was why reading was so good. I could do it quietly and not be too much of a bother.'

God... Aaron's heart broke for her. She'd

been a kid who'd lost her mother. *And* her father, by the sound of it. But she had still felt the need to make herself small—to not be a *bother*. He crouched then without giving the action or how much closer it brought him any thought.

'I'm so sorry,' he said, their eyes meeting now they were on the same level.

She shrugged. 'It is was a long time ago.'

'Did he…is he…?'

Brightening, she closed the book. 'He remarried, when I was in uni. They live in Spain now. I've visited a few times. I'm happy for them. She makes him smile and he deserves to find love again.'

'But?' Aaron definitely detected a *but*.

'Our relationship is…stilted.'

Aaron wasn't surprised, with all that emotional distance her father had laid down. His dad had grieved the break-up of his marriage deeply, and it had toughened him even more, but he hadn't shut his children out. In his own way, he'd pulled them closer. 'I imagine it would be,' he murmured, because he didn't know what else to say.

Trite platitudes about it taking time weren't his style or what she needed.

She shot him a sad, grateful smile, her eyes shimmering with emotion that lurked in the still, brown depths, and Aaron wished he could draw her into his arms and just sit with her in that weird solidarity that came when two people understood intimately what it was to experience loss.

'Anyway.' She gave herself a shake, dropping her gaze to her lap. 'Sorry, I'm prattling on.' Lifting her eyes again, it was as if a veil had come down on the simmer of emotions. 'You have to get going.'

Aaron contemplated telling her she didn't have to pretend she was okay with him, but that felt really personal when she'd been here for two and a half weeks and her life was in boxes back in the UK.

So he stood instead. 'Yeah. My sister's probably already smack-talking about me to the jackaroos. Last time I was late, she told them I was getting a pedicure.'

Her laughter broke the strange tension that had sprung between them. 'Thanks,' she said, looking up at him again. 'For everything.'

Aaron nodded, knowing it wasn't just about the bookcases. 'See you next week.'

Before Chelsea knew it, they were in the last days of November and she'd been part of the OA team for a month. And she *loved* it! Something she announced to Aaron as the plane taxied to a halt back at the base at four o'clock on Thursday afternoon after they'd finished up at a remote health clinic a couple of hundred kilometres west of Balanora.

Unlike the first couple of weeks, they'd worked together a lot this past fortnight— about seventy-five percent of the time—and familiarity had bred *content* as their rapport had developed. She'd been worried about how they would go, given her pulse still did a crazy tap dance every time she saw him, but it seemed that enforced proximity had helped to dull her reaction.

Or at least normalise it. Allow her to put it in perspective. She found him attractive. He found her attractive. It didn't mean *anything* unless they acted upon it. Which meant *they* had the power.

'Love, huh?'

'Yes.' She nodded enthusiastically as she hung up her earphones on the hook and un-buckled. 'The remote clinics remind me why I wanted to be a nurse in the first place.'

He laughed, his hands sliding absently to each end of the stethoscope he had looped around his neck. 'Even with the heat and the flies?'

'Yes.' She hadn't uttered *bloody flies* yet but it had almost slipped out many times.

'What we do out here feels so much more important than what I was doing back home. Let's face it, if you're anywhere near a city or even a town, help—good professional, medical help—is usually not that far away. But out here? We're it. And that means something. I actually feel like I make a difference out here, a real difference.'

'You know you're preaching to the choir, darlin',' Hattie said from behind.

'Amen,' Aaron agreed, his eyes twinkling.

'Yeah, yeah.' Chelsea laughed at herself but the glow of satisfaction inside her chest was too big to suppress. 'It was just a really good day out there, wasn't it?'

There'd been nothing particularly complicated medically—immunisations, wound management, suture removal, baby checks and diabetes management—run of the mill stuff. Their bread and butter. But the fact the forty people at the clinic didn't have to drive over three hours into town and three hours back on dirt roads for basic care, and the *appreciation* that had been evident, had given her a real high.

'It was.' He nodded in acknowledgment. 'It was a good day.'

Then they were smiling at each other,

which felt good too. The hitch in her pulse be damned.

Chelsea was still buoyed an hour later as she restocked the plane. Being in the cool haven of the store room helped, so did her run of three days off stretching ahead. She—*and* Aaron—were on call tonight but that ended at eight a.m. and her days off officially started. Best of all, in the afternoon, Aaron was going to pick her up and take her out to Curran Downs so she could watch the shearing that had started yesterday.

And she was *really* excited about that.

When she entered the front office after the restocking was done, Charmaine and Aaron were debating something at the comms desk. He gestured her over.

'We can't wait for Ju-Ju,' he said to Charmaine as Chelsea approached. 'They're too far out. I'll be fine.'

She shook her head. 'You know them.'

'I know eighty-five percent of the people we see out here, Charmaine.'

'It's Kath. And Dammo. He's one of your oldest friends. They're not just *people*.' Charmaine turned to Chelsea. 'Kath's membranes ruptured and she's gone into premature labour. It's her third pregnancy, a girl. She's twenty-six weeks.'

Bloody hell. Chelsea had hoped she'd get to deliver an Outback baby but not like this.

'She's had an unremarkable antenatal history,' Charmaine continued, 'And both previous children were born at term.'

Chelsea nodded, her midwifery brain rattling through myriad possibilities of how things could go wrong in the middle of nowhere with a very premature baby. On the other hand, the baby could be delivered with no complications at all, or not be born for hours yet, allowing Kath to be safely ensconced in a primary care hospital.

'Her two previous labours were fast,' Aaron added. 'First was two hours. Second was less than an hour on the side of the highway about ten kilometres from town.'

Okay, so maybe time wasn't on their side. 'How far out are they?' she asked.

'Another hundred kilometres west of where we were today,' Aaron supplied.

'It'll take about half an hour in the jet,' Charmaine added.

'Okay.' The jet was fully equipped with a specialised neonatal transport cot that was practically a mini NICU with multiple monitoring devices, pumps and a transport ventilator set up for every eventuality.

'The neonatal team is being dispatched from Brisbane but they're two hours away.'

'Right.' Chelsea threw her bag under the table. 'So we need to go and get Kath.'

'Yes.' Aaron nodded emphatically. 'ASAP. We can get there quicker than Ju-Ju, and the jet is here, ready to go.'

'I know, Aaron. But…are you prepared for a situation where the baby might die out there? A twenty-six-weeker could go either way, you know that. What if she's born not breathing and needs resus and dies anyway, while Dammo is yelling and begging and pleading with you to do something, *anything*, to save her? Are you ready for that? Can you deal with it?'

Chelsea watched the slight bob of Aaron's throat, the angle of his jaw blanching white. Premature labour was always high stakes but, if the couple involved were good friends, everything became personal. He nodded, a grim kind of determination emphasising the battered plains of his face.

'If the worst happens, Dammo's going to need me more than ever. Even if it's some-one to yell at.'

Charmaine glanced at Chelsea. She was obviously torn between looking out for her team and knowing that time was of the essence. She seemed to be asking Chelsea if she was capable not just of dealing with baby delivery but any raw emotional fall-out on an airstrip in the middle of nowhere. Chelsea was no stranger to high emotion in critical situations and, despite having known Aaron for only a month, their connection—acknowledged or not—was such that she felt she could give a slight nod.

'Okay.' Charmaine sighed. 'Fine. But keep me up to date.'

Aaron didn't need to be told twice as he turned to Chelsea. 'Let's go.'

'I can see the vehicle headlights,' Aaron said, his nose plastered to the window. He'd been staring out since the plane had taken off, as if he could will it to their destination faster.

Dammo and Kath had been racing to the airstrip while the plane had been en route and had arrived ten minutes ago. The message from the ground via comms was that Kath's contractions were coming very fast now, which probably meant the baby's arrival was imminent.

While Aaron's leg jiggled and his fingers tapped on his knee, Chelsea went over and over the potential scenarios. They'd set everything up before take-off—the warmer was on in the transport cot and all the appropriate medication had been drawn up and labelled—but preparing mentally for all contingencies was just as important.

'Touchdown in two minutes,' Hattie's calm voice announced in her ears.

The plane banked left and a hit of adrenaline surged into Chelsea's system. She changed channels on her headphone and gestured for Aaron to follow suit. 'You going to be okay?'

'Yes.' His response was curt, his expression intense.

'We have everything ready… We're prepared.'

'Yep.' He nodded but he was less curt this time. 'How many prems have you delivered?'

Chelsea smiled. 'More than I can count on my fingers and toes. And I've assisted in heaps more prem intubations.'

'Good.' He let out a slow breath. 'Don't really get many out here, so it's been a while for me.'

'Don't worry,' she said, a light tease in her voice. 'It's just like a riding a bicycle.'

He gave her a grudging smile as the plane made a bumpy touchdown.

They taxied to the siding and within five minutes Chelsea and Aaron were striding into the heat of an Outback afternoon, nothing but scraggly bush, occasional trees and red dirt beyond the strip for miles and miles. The sound of a woman crying out broke the almost eerie hush, followed by a frantic male voice coming from the vehicle, urging them over.

'Hurry, Aaron. *Hurry!*'

Aaron made it to the back seat of the vehicle where all the action was happening, just ahead of Chelsea. 'Jesus, Kath,' she heard him say. 'You always did like to be the centre of attention.'

Chelsea heard a huffed out laugh but she also heard pain and panic. 'It's too soon,' Kath said, her voice wobbling.

'It's fine,' Aaron assured her. 'We have all the bells and whistles and we're going to get you back to Balanora in a jiffy.'

The calm authority in his voice was just what the situation needed as Chelsea manoeuvred in front of Aaron. 'Hi, Kath, I'm Chelsea.' The labouring woman was half-reclined on the bench seat, supported from behind by a man Chelsea assumed was Dammo. He'd obviously come straight from the paddock, his clothes streaked with dirt and all kinds of stains, and he looked as frantic and helpless as he had sounded.

'Chelsea's a midwife, Kath. And she worked in the NICU for years, so you're in very good hands.'

Slipping into a pair of gloves, Chelsea smiled into the anxious eyes of the panting, sweaty-faced woman. Even with every door open, it was stifling inside the car. 'Do you mind if I have a look and see where you're at?'

Too tired to talk, Kath just nodded. Luckily, she was wearing a skirt and top, which made easing her underwear off much easier, but it was immediately apparent that Chelsea wouldn't need to do an internal examination or use the small hand-held Doppler unit she had stashed in her pocket for listening to the heartbeat. The head was on its way and it wouldn't be long before it crowned.

Whatever state the baby was in, it was coming very, very soon.

'Right.' She patted Kath on the leg. 'Baby's almost here. We need to get you in the plane.'

Just then a contraction cramped through Kath's body and she screwed her face up, clutching at the edge of the seat and groaning, forcing herself to exhale against her body's natural urge to bear down.

Aaron looked at his mate when it passed.

'Pick her up, bring her to the jet and I'll take her at the door.'

Once Kath was settled on the stretcher in the plane, it was action stations. Dammo was at her head and Chelsea at the business end. Aaron checked the suction one more time and put a fine catheter next to Chelsea's hand to use as soon as the baby was born, to clear the airway.

'Kath,' Aaron said. 'I'm going to pop in an IV while you do your thing, okay?'

The woman nodded as he inspected her closest hand, a cannular at the ready. He had it in within seconds and, by the time it was secured, the baby was crowning and then it was born. She was tiny—but bigger than Chelsea had expected—and a bit floppy, but perfect.

'Is she okay?' Kath asked as she pushed herself up onto her elbows to inspect what was happening between her legs. 'Is she breathing?'

'One sec.'

Chelsea could vaguely hear Kath starting to sob and Dammo asking Aaron what was going on, but her entire focus was on the tiny new-born as she sucked the airway, clearing mucous from the baby's nose and mouth.

She was about to ask for a towel as Aaron

said, 'Here,' passing one of the several that had been warming in the transport cot.

Taking it, Chelsea rubbed the baby vigorously—her face and her back—to stimulate breathing. She knew it might not happen, and that she didn't have long before she'd have to hand the baby to Aaron for more potentially drastic measures, but she'd done this often enough to know to start with the basics.

'C'mon, baby,' she whispered as she rubbed. *'C'mon.'*

When the baby took her first gurgling gasp a few seconds later, blinking up at Chelsea, it was the best damned noise she'd ever heard.

'Was that her?' Kath asked, hopefulness rising like a tide in her voice.

'Sure was.' Aaron grinned.

'She's breathing,' Dammo said, his voice tremulous.

'Like a champ,' Aaron confirmed as he handed another warm towel to Chelsea and a tiny pink knitted hat, which she promptly put on, feeling the fontanelles as she did so.

'Bloody hell, mate.' Dammo huffed out a strangled laugh. 'That was the longest thirty seconds of my life.'

Chelsea knew exactly how he felt—time always slowed the longer it took to hear that first new-born wail.

'Hello there, baby girl,' Chelsea crooned at the tiny baby, face screwed up and fully yelling her displeasure now at her rude early delivery. 'Happy birthday. Let's get you some skin-on-skin with your mummy, hey?'

The practice was routine nowadays, but even more vital for premature babies for warmth, protection against infection and to decrease stress levels on a system thrust into the outside world well before it was ready. It obviously wasn't possible for premature babies requiring immediate invasive therapy but, for this bawling little madam, most definitely.

Ordinarily Chelsea would have asked the father if he wanted to cut the cord, but the space was cramped enough, so she quickly clamped and cut before glancing at Aaron. 'Can you do the honours while I finish here?'

Manoeuvring from behind Chelsea, Aaron gently scooped the baby up into hands that were slightly bigger than she was. Inching along the side of the stretcher, he said, 'Kath, I've never seen your boobs before, but I have seen you in a bikini, so let's just pretend we're at the river, okay?'

Kath gave a half-laugh. 'Considering you've seen worse than my boobs today, let's just make a pact that what happens in the plane stays in the plane.'

'Deal.' Aaron grimed. 'Dammo, you want to help lift her shirt so I can slide this little one up under?'

Levering up onto her elbows again, Kath made space for Dammo to pull her T-shirt up at the back as she gathered it up at the front with her non-cannular hand. Aaron gently laid the still squalling infant high up on Kath's chest, her tiny, naked front pressed to her mother's décolletage as he pulled the T-shirt down so the baby's body was fully covered, leaving just her head to stick out through the neck hole of the shirt.

Chelsea, waiting for the birth of the placenta, was only vaguely aware of Aaron adding a couple of warm blankets over the top of the shirt and the sudden, rapid *blip-blip-blip* of the monitor as he connected the saturation probe. Subliminally, she registered that the heart rate was where it should be.

By the time the placenta was delivered, the baby had quietened and Aaron was satisfied with all the vitals—Kath's included. Considering the number of ways it *could* have gone wrong out here in the extreme Outback, the outcome had been spectacular.

The baby—Yolanda—would still need to

be transported to Brisbane for a whole battery of health checks and observations, and would probably stay until she had reached a good weight, but the signs were looking encouraging. Sometimes, of course, premature babies that did well initially could deteriorate and require varying levels of support in the hours and days that followed, which was another good reason to get her to a tertiary hospital.

Within half an hour of Yolanda's birth, they were taking off again, the newest addition to the Balanora district still snuggled skin-to-skin with her mother, her heart beat pinging reassuringly over the background hum of the cabin. Dammo was in the seat behind the stretcher, leaning forward, his chin tucked in next to Kath's temple as they admired their baby girl.

Chelsea was at the foot of the stretcher facing Kath and the monitor and Aaron was in his usual seat, diagonally opposite and directly across the narrow aisle from his mate. But he wasn't looking out of the window any more, he was looking at Chelsea, grinning at her, clearly thrilled with their accomplishment.

As was she, feeling the solidarity of the moment acutely.

Feeling it, and *other* things, in the hitch of her breath, the loop of her stomach, the kick in her pulse. Feeling it in the ache of her face as she grinned right back.

CHAPTER SEVEN

CHELSEA WAS STILL feeling the high from last night when Aaron picked her up the next day after lunch for their trip to Currans Downs. She definitely felt it when she climbed in the cab of his blessedly cool ute and he said, 'Hey.'

His hair was all tousled around his head, as if he'd just shoved his fingers through it this morning and called it done, and his face creased into a smile of welcome. He was all relaxed and loose, and looked perfectly at home in the ute, his Akubra—almost as battered as his face—stashed on the dashboard.

It wasn't that he didn't look relaxed and loose at work, but it was different, and she wasn't sure she'd get used to the contrast between the laidback flight doctor with the stethoscope slung around his neck and the weekend sheep farmer in work shorts, sturdy boots and a flannel shirt rolled up to his elbows. They were both a sight to behold, but the guy in the ute had an ease about him that was overwhelmingly masculine.

And that connection from last night fizzed anew.

'Hi.'

'You ready for a day of roustabouting?'

Chelsea laughed. She had no clue what it was but she was in. 'Bring it on, buddy.' If only calling him *buddy* would make those acute feelings of connection disappear.

'Dammo rang this morning,' he said as they headed on the highway out of town.

'Yeah?' She'd been wondering how things had gone after they'd transferred all three occupants to the Brisbane jet that had been waiting on the tarmac for them when they'd got to base. She glanced at his profile. 'How's Yolanda doing? And Kath?'

'They're doing well.' He kept his eyes on the road. 'Going like a trooper, apparently. Her condition has remained stable. They inserted a nasogastric tube, because she's not strong enough yet to suck adequately or for very long periods of time, but hopefully she'll stack on some weight quickly and be able to feed properly before too much longer.'

Chelsea nodded. The benefits of breastfeeding increased exponentially with premature babies. 'Did they say what her weight was?'

'Nine hundred and fifty-two grams.'

'Wow.' She laughed out loud. 'Nearly a kilo. I thought she looked a decent size for a twenty-six-weeker. No wonder she coped well with her early outing.'

'Yep, it certainly helped.'

'They were lucky, though.' Chelsea returned her gaze to the windscreen and the haze of heat rising up ahead. The long, arrow-straight road seemed to disappear into the shimmering distance. 'If she'd been smaller, if there'd been something inherently wrong causing the premature labour, if she'd needed reviving, it could have been really hairy.'

'God, I know. I gave myself nightmares thinking of all the possibilities last night.'

Chelsea smiled as the pocket in the back of her knee-length denim shorts buzzed and she remembered she'd stashed her phone there as she'd left the house. Leaning forward, she reached behind to grab it, conscious suddenly that Aaron's gazed skimmed the dip of her back and the rise of her buttocks before returning his attention to the road.

Her nipples prickled against the fabric of

her bra and, befuddled, she had to tap in her code twice. A text alert sat on the bottom of the screen. From Francesca. She almost didn't answer it until Aaron said, 'That was lucky. Won't be long before the signal runs out.'

And then Chelsea *had* to look, just in case it was something important. Francesca's texting had settled after those first few days and she didn't like to let them go unanswered for too long.

Chelsea opened the text and immediately wished she hadn't as a picture of Alfie appeared on the screen. So like Dom. Dom's dark eyes, fringed with Dom's long, dark eyelashes, smiling Dom's irreverent smile into the camera. It kicked her in the chest as per usual.

Alfie says hi.

She couldn't do anything for long moments, just stare at the picture. It had been so good this past month, not having a constant reminder of Alfie around. After the high of last night, it brought her back to earth with a thud.

Aaron's, 'Cute kid,' broke her out of her funk. 'That a nephew? Or a friend's child?'

Chelsea stared so hard at the picture, her eyes almost watered. 'No.' She shook her head. 'It's Dom's son.'

'Oh. I...didn't know he had a child.'

Chelsea could hear the frown in his voice as well as the hesitancy as she looked up from the phone screen and met his soft gaze. 'I didn't either until a year ago.'

Glancing back at the road, he didn't say anything for a beat or two. 'How old is he?'

'Almost four.'

More silence but, studying his profile as she was, Chelsea could practically see his mental arithmetic. A man who'd been dead for three years had a four-year-old son his widow didn't know about. 'Okay, that...'

He halted, as if thinking better of what he was going to say, his lips pressing together. But Chelsea wanted to know. 'What?'

'It's fine.' He shook his head. 'It's not my business. You don't have to talk about it.'

Chelsea had no idea why she'd told him. But Francesca killing her buzz had stirred up feelings that had receded since she'd arrived and she realised she *did* want to talk—finally.

She hadn't talked to anyone about the impact of Alfie, because she knew no one who hadn't also known Dom and hadn't been touched by his death. So she'd just locked it all down. But suddenly it felt too big to ignore.

And Aaron, it seemed, was her confessional. She'd already told him stuff about her mum and dad that she'd never told another living soul. What was one more steaming chunk of emotional baggage from Chelsea's past?

Maybe it was because of how removed Aaron was. Maybe it was because she knew he understood what it was like to not feel *enough*. Maybe there was another reason she didn't want to examine too closely. All Chelsea knew was she *wanted* to tell him.

'I'm okay to talk about it.'

He flicked a glance at her, as if to check she actually meant it. Their eyes met briefly and she saw the nanosecond he understood she *was* okay. Looking back at the road, he said, 'So Dom…'

His voice drifted off and Chelsea could tell he was trying to find a word that was palatable. 'Cheated on me?' Chelsea raised both her eyebrows. 'Yes.'

His knuckles tightened around the steering wheel. 'With Alfie's mother.'

'Amongst others, yes.'

Shooting her a quick alarmed look, he said, *'Others?'*

'Yeah.' She turned her gaze back to the endless road in front of them and the even more endless paddocks of stubbly grass and occasional flocks of scraggly sheep. 'He'd been dead for eight months when I learned about Shari. She was the first one. Via email.'

Aaron winced. 'Bloody hell.'

Yep. 'She'd been going through the AA steps and had got to the making amends part. She decided that she'd wronged me by sleeping with my husband while he was in Afghanistan and she had to confess to move on.'

'That was *nice* of her.'

Chelsea gave a half-laugh at the sarcasm in his voice. 'I confronted Vinnie about it. That's Dom's brother. They served in the same unit so they always deployed together. He denied that Dom had ever been unfaithful. He said that Shari, who worked for the British embassy in Kabul, was known for her dalliances with anything in a uniform, and that Dom had rebuffed her several times, which had left her bitter. He begged me not to tell Francesca, their mother.'

'You believed him?'

'Yes.' She nodded slowly. 'Ninety-five percent. But it niggled, you know?'

'Uh-huh.'

'Then, a year ago, Krystal turned up on

our doorstep in Hackney with Alfie. She'd been a nanny for a British official in Kandahar. Dom apparently didn't know she'd had his child.'

'So why did she suddenly decide to turn up out of the blue like that?'

'Her life circumstances had changed and she'd fallen on hard times, and was at her wits' end with nowhere else to go. Vinnie was angry, denying Alfie could be Dom's kid, and Francesca was equally adamant, and they insisted on a DNA test but... I didn't need one.'

'You knew?' He glanced across at her.

'No. Well...' Chelsea huffed out a laugh. 'Yes, I guess I did. That five percent of me did. But Alfie is the *spitting image* of Dom. I don't know how his family could look at that little boy and possibly deny it. So there was *zero* doubt in my mind.'

'What happened then?'

'The DNA test came back positive—of course—and I confronted Vinnie again, said it was time to stop protecting Dom and that I needed to know the truth. About all his women. Because part of me knew there'd be more. I don't know why I wanted to know. I mean, what good could it possibly do? I'm pretty sure Vinnie felt the same but I *needed* to know.'

'I get that.'

'He blustered around a bit at first. I don't blame him for trying to protect his brother. He was there when Dom died and I know he suffers from terrible survivor guilt. But I was in such a fury at that point that I threatened to tell Francesca about the email from two years ago and he came clean.'

'And there *were* others.'

'Yes. Apparently, the man I loved, and worried about dying over there every single, waking second of the day, was a bit of a man whore when he was deployed.'

'Oh God, Chelsea.' He looked away from the road for a beat or two. 'I am so sorry.'

His gaze was brief before switching back to the road again but it was intense, radiating empathy. The look she'd seen many times these past weeks as Aaron had interacted with patients.

'Vinnie tried to explain the mentality of being deployed in a war zone. How having to confront your own mortality day after day often led to fatalistic behaviour. Living each day like it was your last. Dom loved me, he said, and his liaisons weren't about love, they were about sex.'

'Did it help?'

Chelsea gave a harsh laugh. 'Not really.'

'You must be pretty angry with him.'

She was about to say she was furious but, actually, she wasn't sure she was any more. Not like she had been. She was just…sad. 'I was.'

'I guess it's hard to mourn someone, to love someone, when they hurt you so deeply.'

'I don't love him.'

Chelsea blinked. It was the first time she'd said it out loud. Her instinct to take it back was strong but she pressed her lips together tight. She glanced across at Aaron, who didn't appear to be horrified by her disloyalty to her dead husband, or annoyed that she'd let him think otherwise that day in the store room when she'd not refuted it.

'I mean… I'm not *in* love with him any more. There's part of me that will always love him. Dom was a massive part of my life for many years but…however he justified it to himself, however much I understand how Vinnie justifies it… Dom betrayed me and our vows and the things I held most sacred. And that just…killed off any deep feelings I had for him. Snuffed them right out.'

A slight rise in the road levelled out to reveal three large red kangaroos up ahead, sitting in the middle of the road. They were far enough away for Aaron to slow, which he did, but the sight never failed to thrill Chelsea. If ever she temporarily forgot she was in a vastly different land, the appearance of kangaroos always brought her back to reality. She'd seen a lot out here, both hopping through paddocks as planes landed or stinking everything up as road kill, but she didn't think she'd ever get used to the sight of the strange, quirky creatures.

They hopped away before the ute even got close and Aaron accelerated away again. He hadn't said anything about her declaration and she wondered if she'd shocked him. Sighing, she rolled her head to one side to study his profile.

'I suppose that makes me a terrible person,' she murmured, not wanting to leave their conversation dangling.

'No longer being in love with the man who repeatedly cheated on you?' Aaron shook his head as he glanced across at her. 'I'd say it makes you human.'

If there could possibly have been a right answer to her question, Aaron had nailed it, and the niggling sense of guilt Chelsea too often felt over her conflicted feelings eased back.

'Who sent it to you? The picture. Are you…in contact with Alfie's mother?'

'No.' Chelsea sighed again. 'Francesca sent it.'

'Your *mother-in-law* sent you a picture of the child your *husband* had with *another* woman?'

Chelsea almost laughed at the streak of disbelief in Aaron's voice. It did sound kind of unbelievable when spoken out loud. 'Alfie and Krystal lived with us for four months until she got back on her feet.'

'What?'

She did laugh this time. 'Yeah. I know. It seems bizarre, but Francesca and Roberto had their first grandchild from their dead son, and they weren't about to turn her or him away.'

'Wasn't that hard?'

'Oh, yes.' Chelsea nodded, fixing her gaze on the ever-present heat shimmer ahead. 'Very much so. Dom and I… We had two miscarriages after we'd been married for a few years. The first pregnancy was an accident but the second was planned. When we lost that one too, we decided to give it a rest. Dom was about to be deployed again and we talked about leaving it until after he got out of the military.'

It was hard to keep the emotion of those years out of her voice so Chelsea didn't even try. It had been a long time, but sometimes the searing loss of that period returned with a roaring vengeance.

'So, yeah…' She came out of her reverie, turning her head to focus on Aaron. 'Having to look at a kid that was a replica of Dom, a child that *I* couldn't give him, was hard. Living with the woman who had slept with my husband was hard. Thankfully Krystal got back on her feet and moved out but Francesca and Roberto look after Alfie in the afternoons so she can work, and he usually stays over one night on the weekend.'

'Bloody hell. Do they understand how hard that must be for you?'

'No. They don't see Dom's infidelity when they look at Alfie. They just see… Dom. And they think that I'll love Alfie too because I love Dom—*loved* Dom—and he's Dom's, therefore…' Chelsea shook her head at the convoluted but understandable logic. 'And I do love him. He's a sweet, *sweet* boy, who wormed his way into all our hearts, and none of this is his fault. But…well, let's just say, it's been nice to get away from all that.'

'I bet.' Aaron shook his head. 'Why don't you ask her to stop sending you pictures?'

'Because she's trying to keep me connected and because he's her grandson and
she adores him. And she doesn't know that it
hurts because I've never told her. She doesn't
know the extent of Dom's liaisons. She thinks
that Krystal was a one-off. And that I've forgiven him because he's dead. And I'm not
going to be the one to tell her that it wasn't,
and I haven't, because it'll break her heart
and it's already been broken enough.'

Chelsea knew how it felt to lose two babies
at a point where neither were much more than
a collection of cells. She couldn't begin to
image the pain of losing a child who had been
a part of your life for over three decades.

'So you just…suck it up. Even though it
hurts?'

God, he made her sound like some kind of
martyr. It didn't sit comfortably, but it was
what it was. 'Yeah.'

Aaron glanced at her incredulously. 'Why?'

'Because sometimes we lie to people we
love to protect them, even if it makes us feel
bad.'

'Yeah but…' He turned his attention back
to the road. 'Isn't it okay to put yourself first
at some point?'

'Sure.' And she'd done that. 'It's why I
moved here.'

'So…' He slid her another look. 'You *are* running away.'

Chelsea smiled. 'I prefer to think of it as starting over.' She quirked an eyebrow. 'Surely that can be added to your list of reasons people come out here?'

He nodded slowly. 'Yeah. Okay. Consider the list updated.'

She laughed then, and the heaviness that had descended in the cabin lifted. Up ahead, a sign announced a road off to the left, and Aaron slowed the ute and indicated.

'Hold on to your hat,' he said as the car slowed. 'The road gets kinda bumpy from here in out.'

After several hours in the heat of the sheering shed, the stifling air thick with the earthy aromas of lanolin, sheep droppings and sweat, Chelsea's admiration for Aaron and anyone trying to make a living off the land out here grew exponentially. The fact that he was busily striding around in those boots, those shorts, that hat and just a navy singlet now, after discarding his flannel shirt, didn't hurt.

Rock music pumped through rusty old speakers mounted in the corners of the shed as he cajoled sheep and whistled at dogs and flapped away the ever-present flies and lifted fleece, spreading it out on the wool table to class it then toss it in the presser. He was everywhere and Chelsea could barely keep up as he explained and demonstrated and encouraged her to get dirty.

If she hadn't been heavily in lust with him already, she was now.

Although, it was more than just those sun-kissed muscles straining and bending and stretching and contracting and *sweating*. It was the way he laughed and joked with the shearers, as though they'd known him all his life, and the way he teased his sister, who was also bustling around, yet clearly deferred to her, and the respect he showed his father, while bantering with him about getting old and retiring.

He was clearly as at home here, a broom in his hand, as he was in the belly of a King Air, a stethoscope around his neck, and Chelsea's heart skipped so many beats over the course of the afternoon she started to worry she was developing a condition.

Just before knock-off time, the four-shearer team members—who had already sheared over two hundred sheep each—plus Aaron and his sister had a friendly race to see who could shear the fastest. Mostyn Vincent, sporting the same lived-in kind of face as his son, pulled a stopwatch out of his back pocket as if it was a common occurrence during shearing time and, with all six of them hunched over a sheep, called, *'Go!'*

Chelsea watched as the electrical hum of shears and the hands and legs and instruments all worked in tandem to methodically strip off the fleece in one piece. All four of the pros finished within a few seconds of each other. Aaron and Tracey brought up the rear several minutes later, with Tracey just pipping her brother to the post.

'Now who's the old man?' Mostyn crowed.

Aaron laughed as he finished off the sheep and came up for a high-five from his sister.

'It's those soft hands,' Ed, the team boss, said which earned more laughs all round.

'You want a go?' Aaron asked, his eyes meeting hers.

Chelsea blinked. 'Me?'

'Sure.' He grinned at her as he swiped a muscular forearm over his sweaty brow. 'I'll teach you.'

She glanced at the faces around her to see if this was some kind of set-up. 'Um…'

Before she could get any more out, Ed made *bok-bok-bok* noises and she rolled her eyes at him, which earned her a hoot of laughter. 'What if I...cut the sheep?'

'You won't. I'll be right beside you,' Aaron assured her. 'Where's your sense of adventure?'

Chelsea narrowed her eyes at him but he grinned and she said, 'Okay, fine.'

Before she could blink, she was being ushered to a shearing station as Ed went and got her a sheep. 'Here you are, English, got you a nice docile one.'

The guys on the team had been teasing her all afternoon about her accent and Chelsea laughed as the sheep was positioned between her legs. It felt hot and heavy against her thighs, but there was little time to register that as Aaron turned on the shears and started talking her through the steps.

The shears felt weighty and foreign in her hands and they vibrated like crazy as Chelsea hunched over the sheep and made her first pass on the finer belly fleece as instructed. A little black fly buzzed around the sweat forming on her upper lip and she blew at it, but it was still less distracting then Aaron, who was also hunched over, his body close to hers, his mouth close to her ear so she could hear his pointers.

Even though they were being watched by

six other people, it felt as if it were just the two of them. The deep husk of his voice, the warmth of his breath fluffing the flyaway wisps of hair plastered to her neck, the way he occasionally leaned closer, helping her manoeuvre the sheep or showing her how to angle the shears, felt strangely intimate.

Concentrating hard on what she was doing so she didn't nick the poor sheep, she wasn't even aware that she'd muttered, 'Bloody flies,' as she blew another one—or maybe it was the same one—away.

Aaron's warm chuckle drifted down her neck. 'I heard that, *English*, but don't worry, your secret is safe with me.'

Chelsea actually shivered, despite the heat, her concentration officially shot. Standing, she clicked off the shears and stretched out her back. It had been a physically demanding afternoon and she could already feel a niggle in her lumbar area from just a few minutes hunched over.

'Okay, I'm calling it,' she said. 'This is not for the faint of heart.'

Ed grinned. 'Step aside, English, let me show you how it's done.'

Chelsea and Aaron moved over to where Tracey and Mostyn stood and left Ed to it. 'You okay?' he asked.

'Yep.' She nodded. 'I have a feeling I'm going to be sore tomorrow, though.'

'Oh, trust me,' Tracey said. 'You're going to have aches and pains in places you never knew you had muscles.'

'Hey,' Aaron mock-protested. 'Way to kill the adventure buzz.'

Tracey grinned. 'You want to come up to the homestead and take a bath?' she asked Chelsea. 'Get out of those sweaty clothes before dinner?'

'Or,' Aaron suggested, 'She could have an open-air shower at the shearers' digs.'

Chelsea glanced at Tracey who almost imperceptibly shook her head before saying, 'Yeah, tough choice. A long, deep soak for aching bones and muscles with a luxury bath bomb and divine-smelling soap and shampoo… Or a cold shower in a hessian-wrapped cubicle from a bag hanging off a tree branch, a bunch of rowdy blokes nearby belly-aching at you to finish up, and the birdlife dive-bombing you.'

Aaron laughed. 'That only happened to you once.'

What? She might be all about the adventure but bird attack whilst showering did not appeal. Chelsea glanced at Tracey. 'Thanks. A bath sounds lovely.'

'You don't know what you're missing out,'
Aaron said.

Chelsea shrugged. 'Maybe next time.'

As soon as it was out she wanted to withdraw it, but Aaron smiled at her reply as if
he hoped there *would* be a next time, and she
couldn't help but hope the same.

CHAPTER EIGHT

Three hours later, Aaron pulled the ute up in the middle of a paddock and killed the headlights, immediately engulfing them in darkness.

'Here?' Chelsea asked after a beat or two, as she peered out of the windscreen and then her window into the inky black of the night.

'Yep.'

She looked around again, as if she'd been expecting stadium seating. 'The best place is near the river, but it's a bit further away, and all we need is to be far enough from the lights of the homestead.'

Unclicking his seat belt, Aaron opened the door, because the temptation to reach for her after their amazing day together was too great. Between how she enthusiastically and uncomplainingly pitched in at the shearing shed, to the way she'd got on with his family, to her easy conversation and witty banter throughout dinner, she'd been building like a drum beat in his blood.

This very English woman just seemed to fit in to this very Aussie setting.

The air was still warm but the sting of the day had dissipated as he strode round to the tray of the ute and grabbed the blanket. Ordinarily, for star-gazing he'd have thrown a mattress in the back, but he didn't want Chelsea to think he'd lured her out here under false pretences.

After today, he was starting to understand his feelings went deeper than how sexy she looked in the strappy dress she was now wearing, or how tempting it was to pull out the band in her hair and let it all fall loose.

Chelsea had been through a lot, and if she really was here not because she was running away but to start over—to *stay*—then they had time to explore whatever *this* was. Because he was sure he wasn't alone in these feelings and he didn't want to screw anything up by going too hard too fast.

She was still sitting in the cab of the car as he came round her side and he smiled to himself as he opened the door. 'Scared of the dark?'

Peering out at him, she blinked. 'I'm not sure I've *been* anywhere this dark.'

He laughed and held out his hand. 'Yeah, moon won't be up for a few more hours. Great? Isn't it?'

The unclicking of her seatbelt sounded loud in the cacophony of silence around them, then her hand slid into his. 'Are we lying on the ground?' she asked as he guided her to the front of the vehicle.

'No.' Aaron threw the blanket on the bonnet of the car. 'We're sitting up here. Best seats in the house.' He shoved his booted foot onto the lower rung of the bull bar and hauled himself up, before turning and offering his hand once again. 'You coming?'

A minute later they were sitting side by side—not touching but still close—their legs stretched out in front of them, the blanket beneath protecting them from the heat of the engine, reclining against the windscreen he'd washed thoroughly when Chelsea had been in the bath.

'Wow,' she whispered as she craned her neck to take in the sky from horizon to horizon.

Aaron smiled at the awe in that one hushed word. 'Yeah.'

Above him a wonderland glimmered and dazzled. Planets and suns and constellations. Far-away galaxies. All blending together to form the rich tapestry of lights making up the great southern night sky.

'Do you know what any of these stars are called?'

'Some.'

He pointed them out then and they whiled away half an hour talking about all things celestial, Chelsea mostly listening, Aaron mostly talking. But Aaron was hyper-aware of *her*. Every breath, every move. Every brush of her arm against his. Every turn of her head as she glanced at his profile. Every adjustment of that one errant strap that kept sliding down her arm. Every shake of her shoulders as she laughed at something he said.

His entire body thrummed with awareness. With the slow, thick beat of his blood and the hot, heavy flow of his breath.

And then she said, 'You know, the first date Dom ever took me on was to the Planetarium at the Royal Observatory.'

It was kind of a mood killer.

Aaron had believed her today when she'd said she wasn't in love with her husband any more. And it had been like a weight off his chest—one he didn't even know he'd been carrying. So the very last name he wanted to hear on her lips tonight was *Dom*.

But it made sense that lying here under the stars would trigger the memory, particularly given how recently they'd spoken about him. And he didn't want to be that guy—a douche about the men in a woman's past.

'How'd you meet?'

She stared into the night sky. 'I was at uni in London and he and the lads from his unit used to drink at a pub me and my girlfriends used to frequent.'

Keeping his eyes firmly overhead, he said, 'And was it love at first sight?'

She gave a little laugh. 'Good lord, no. He was quite the lothario which, in retrospect, should have been a heads-up.' She laughed again, a shallow echo of the first. 'Sure, I found him attractive, and he kept asking me out, but he was always there with a different girl. He just seemed like a player to me and I wasn't interested in being a notch on anyone's bedpost.'

'But?' There obviously *was* a but—they'd married, after all.

'He was persistent. Not creepily so. Charmingly. And I was so used to being a…ghost at home. Being seen, being wanted, being *pursued*…that was a revelation. Dom gave affection so easily and freely without me having to silently beg for it. I wasn't used to that from a man, so it was hard to trust initially, but when I did, well…it was heady stuff.'

Aaron shut his eyes. Jesus. Poor Chelsea, starved for attention. No wonder she'd fallen for Dom. 'And now?' He glanced across at her, his eyes well and truly adjusted to the night, his gaze following the line of her profile. 'Did Dom's infidelity make you distrustful of men again?'

Surely it had to have had some impact?

She shook her head as she turned her head to look at him. 'It made me mistrust *myself*. But mostly it made me feel…'

The silence grew between them. 'Feel…?' he prompted.

Glancing away, she huffed out a breath. 'It doesn't matter.'

'You can say it, you know,' he murmured, his gaze trained on her profile. 'It's just you and me and the stars.'

Aaron saw the bob of her throat, heard her swallow, heard the rough exhale, and waited. 'It reinforced how I've always felt. Like… I wasn't enough. Not enough for my dad to love me. Not enough for my husband to be faithful to me. Just…' Her voice roughened and her throat bobbed again. 'Not enough.'

The utter dejection in her voice cut Aaron to his core. 'Hey,' he said, rolling onto his side, sliding his hand onto her cheek and into her hair. 'I'm sorry. I'm *so* sorry that happened to you, Chelsea. And that people you loved and trusted made you feel that way.'

Turning on her side, she shot him a sad smile. 'It's okay, you don't have to—'

'Yes,' he interrupted. 'I do.' Someone had to. It was a tragedy that she felt so unworthy, and his chest ached with the unfairness of it because, while his mother leaving had left him feeling similarly, he'd had other people around him—people who loved him—telling him, *showing* him, otherwise.

His hand held firmer in her hair. 'You are enough, Chelsea Tanner. You are *more* than enough. You've been with the OA for a month and there's not one person on the team that wouldn't say the same thing. And any guy who was lucky enough to be in a position to tell you that, and didn't spend every single second of his life doing so, has a lot to answer for. I'm sorry you weren't loved the way you deserve to be loved.'

The way he wanted to love her. Because he *was* falling in love with her—he knew it as surely as he knew the sun would rise over this ancient landscape tomorrow.

Even though she was everything he'd avoided all his life.

She stared at him then as if she didn't know what to say. Aaron didn't know what to say either so he leaned in and kissed her instead.

She tasted sweet, like the golden syrup she'd smothered all over the warm damper they'd had for dessert, and she smelled like whatever the hell had been in that fancy bath bomb Tracey had supplied. Vanilla or orange or passion fruit. Something edible which had driven him crazy throughout dinner. Her lips were soft and pliant, and the small moan that came from somewhere at the back of her throat unleashed a tsunami of lust that Aaron's better angels had been keeping under wraps for what felt like for ever.

His pulse pumped through his chest, his belly and his groin, and he was only vaguely aware of the loud rasp of his breath as he opened his mouth and deepened the kiss, groaning when she did the same.

Then, somehow, she was closer. Or maybe he was. Had she moved, or had he? Had they both moved? Aaron wasn't sure. All he knew was the tips of her breasts were rubbing his chest, her knees were brushing his lower thighs and his hand was dropping from her hair, running down her spine to the dip at the small of her back and palming her butt, urging her closer.

Urging her in all the way.

Until her breasts were flattened and their thighs were smooshed and their hips were aligned and there was no way she could not feel the *full* effect of what kissing her was doing to his body.

It wasn't anything like the two kisses they'd already shared. They'd been rash and brief, halted abruptly out of surprise and a sense of transgression. A sense of being wrong.

This didn't feel wrong. It felt like the culmination of what this day had been leading to. What this past month had been leading to.

Hell, out here under the stars, it felt like their freaking destiny.

But, as her kiss plunged deeper and her knee slid between his legs, her thigh pressing against the almost agonising thickness of his erection, Aaron knew if he didn't stop now it was going to be a lot more than just some first-base action on the bonnet of his ute.

It was going to be a home run.

And that would be the very definition of going too hard, too fast. He was a thirty-five-year-old man, not a horny teenager, and he'd waited for this—for *her*—all his damned life.

He didn't want to mess up because he let his libido have the con.

Libidos weren't generally known for their detailed decision-making process. Gathering every skerrick of his willpower, Aaron pulled out of the kiss. He didn't go far, just pressing his forehead against hers, their rough pants mingling together.

'Aaron?' she asked, her voice small. 'Everything okay?'

God…she sounded as befuddled as he felt. 'Everything is perfect,' he assured her, nuzzling her temple now.

'You…don't want this?'

He shut his eyes. 'Oh, I want it.' He chugged out a laughed as he tipped his head back a little to look at her. 'I'm just trying to be…' God…what? Restrained? Gentlemanly? Respectful? 'I don't want you to think I brought you out here for this.'

She didn't say anything for a moment, then she moved the leg she had jammed between them, causing his breath to hitch and a mini-eruption in his groin. Sliding it over the top of his thigh, she rolled herself up, pressing on his upper shoulder as she went, displacing him onto his back.

By the time she was settled, she was straddling him, the centre of her pressing into the bulge behind his fly. His hands had come to rest on her legs mid-thigh, his palms on warm, bare skin, his fingers on the hem of her dress. Her strap had slipped again but she didn't bother fixing it this time.

'I don't think that.'

'Good.' Aaron was mollified to hear she didn't doubt his motives. His libido, however, didn't care about his motives, it only cared about how good it felt to have her atop him and how easy it would be to push his hands under the fabric of her dress…

'But I'm okay to be going there anyway.'

If she'd applied a cattle prod to his erection, it couldn't have bucked harder than it did and, by the way she shifted, he was pretty sure she'd felt it too. He swallowed. 'Okay.'

She stared down at him for long moments. 'No one had ever said that to me, before… the sorry thing. *Sorry that happened to you, Chelsea.* Not my father. Not Francesca or Vinnie. It means a lot.'

Aaron's pulse thudded thick through his head as an uneasy feeling took up residence in the pit of the stomach. 'So this is a…thank you?'

'What?' She frowned and shook her head. 'No.'

A very distracting piece of hair slid from

her up-do to kiss her nape. Aaron's fingers itched to play with it and he dug them into her thighs to suppress the impulse.

'This is… I didn't know I could feel like this. And…' She paused, as if she was searching for the right words. 'I'm so lucky to have shared this day with you. And… I'm attracted to you, and have been since the room mix up at the hotel, and all this…' She looked up and then back at him. 'Makes me want to do something wild and free, and I haven't wanted to do that with *anyone* for a very long time, but I want to do it with you.'

A well of emotion stormed his chest, each word sliding inside his heart, and Aaron knew that whatever happened with them he'd never forget this night underneath the stars, falling in love with Chelsea.

'Well… I can't fault your logic,' he said with a grin, because this wasn't the moment for such a grand declaration.

She grinned too, momentarily, before reaching for the hem of her dress and pulling it up and off her head, leaving her in nothing but a white pair of panties.

'Holy mother of…' Aaron whispered, his pulse spiking, his gaze fixed on the lush curves of her bare breasts and the pebbled nipples at each centre.

Then she reached up and pulled at the band in her hair and it cascaded down in fine wisps. Christ…she was magnificent. Incandescent against the backdrop of the Milky Way, crowned in a garland of stars.

His hands moved then, sliding up her thighs, glancing over her belly and her ribs to each capture a breast, thumbs stroking across the engorged nipples in unison. Damn if his hands didn't look *good* on her. Big and tanned and a little rough against the pale creaminess of her skin, but *good*.

She moaned and arched her back, and Aaron vaulted up, his mouth landing on her throat as he kneaded the soft flesh, and she rocked against him.

'God,' she gasped as she tugged at his shirt. 'Please tell me you have a condom.'

It took a moment for Aaron to think through the heavy haze buzzing through his system as Chelsea yanked his shirt free of his head and tossed it. 'Wallet. Back pocket.'

But for damned sure they were going to need more than one.

It had been such a long time since a man had held her in his arms like this and Chelsea realised how much she'd missed it as she groped for the wallet. She hadn't for the longest time. Dom's betrayal had torpedoed the intimacy they'd shared and knocked her libido flat. But, in this small dot on an Outback map, it had suddenly roared to form and life and had a name.

'Aaron,' she whispered as his lips drifted south, and his heat, his earthiness, his closeness overwhelmed her.

He made a low humming noise, his hot, wet mouth replacing the fingers toying with a nipple, and Chelsea cried out, her hand fumbling with the square piece of leather she'd somehow managed to wrangle from his pocket. Her head fell back, the action thrusting her breasts out, and Aaron took ruthless advantage, ravaging them with such skill, Chelsea was lost to everything but the flick of his tongue and the pull of his mouth.

At some point, he lifted his head and panted, 'Condom,' before going right back to his deliberations.

With monumental effort Chelsea got back on task, lifting her head to riffle through his wallet, thanking God for her night vision as her ability to coordinate dissolved under the play of Aaron's tongue and the fine rub of his whiskers that prickled *everywhere*.

Locating the condom, Chelsea almost brandished it up high and called out *Huzzah!* But she chose to conserve her energy for what was to come. Sliding her hands onto the smooth acreage of his shoulders, she pressed more urgently against the bulge in his shorts and started to rub. Sensation flared between her hips and she let out a strangled kind of moan at the same time as Aaron's guttural grunt.

His mouth slipped from her nipple as his hand clamped down hard on the small of her back. 'Chelsea…' He puffed out a strangled kind of laugh into the hollow at the base of her throat. 'That'll end messily if you keep doing that.'

The fact that Aaron seemed to be as out of control, as close to the edge, as she did, quashed any thoughts hovering in the back of her mind about her lack of *practice*. Sliding a hand into the rich layers of his hair, she tilted his head back until they were staring into each other's eyes. It might have been dark but his gaze was utterly transparent. She saw desire—*lust*—but also emotion, something that went beyond this crazy, desperate need thrumming between them.

Something deeper.

Chelsea supposed she should feel exposed, embarrassed even, about sharing her deepest, darkest hurts with this man. But sitting next to him in this deepest, darkest night, knowing he too knew something about loss and inadequacy, felt…right.

She kissed him then, her lips opening over his, her hand sliding to his jaw, the rasp of his whiskers against her palm hardening her nipples. Her belly looped then tightened as her pulse fluttered at her temples, wrists and between her legs. His tongue brushed hers and Chelsea moaned as she returned the favour, tangling with him in a delicious dance. Her head filled with the taste of him, the smell of him. Eucalyptus and leather and petrichor.

Panting, she pulled out of the kiss. Part of her wanted to do nothing but keep her lips locked with his all night, but parts *lower* were demanding more. A fever burned thought her blood and only Aaron—hard and good and deep inside her—could break it.

Chelsea shifted slightly as she handed him the condom. 'Open this,' she requested as she reached for his fly.

The sound of husky breathing, the tearing of foil and the rip of a zipper all seemed amplified in the absolute silence of the landscape. Unlike Aaron's, 'Oh, Jesus,' which hovered rough and low around them as Chelsea finally liberated his erection from his underwear.

He felt good in her hand. Long and thick

and solid as Chelsea closed her fingers around him, stroking up and down, familiarising herself with his contours, revelling in the shudder rippling through his body. He groaned again, his forehead pressing into the crook of her neck, his breath hot as he pushed her hand aside, muttering, 'Mercy, woman,' as he rolled the sheath down his length.

Chelsea's pulse accelerated as she pressed closer to Aaron once more, reaching for his hardness with one hand, pushing the gusset of her underwear out the way with the other. Lifting her hips slightly, she looked into his upturned face. The thick, blunt prod of him nudged her entrance as his hands slid to the small of her back. Their slight roughness caused her nipples to bead and Chelsea's entire body pulsed in anticipation.

'When you say you haven't done this for a very long time,' he said, his voice husky, his expression earnest. 'You mean…?'

'Not since Dom,' she confirmed.

He nodded slowly. 'Do you need me to…?'

Chelsea wasn't sure what he was going to say, but she didn't give him a chance to finish. She just sank down—not fast, but not slow either—in a measured, deliberate move that filled her all the way to the hilt, stealing the breath from her lungs and causing Aaron to gasp.

She clutched him to her chest, her arms wrapping around his head and shoulders, his arms wrapping around her waist as she breathed steadily through the thick intrusion stretching her so damned good.

'You okay?' he asked after a beat or two.

'Yeah, just…' Her arms tightened around him as she adjusted to his girth and depth. 'Give me a second.'

A wave of emotion rolled from the pit of her stomach all the way to her throat. She'd felt so broken for so long and in a handful of weeks this man, in a place on the other side of the planet, had put her back together. Or at least, shown her that it was possible to be whole again.

He chuckled. 'Take as long as you want. We could just stay like this all night and I'd be totally down with that.'

Chelsea gave a husky laugh. 'I think you mean…' She undulated internal muscles. 'Up.'

He sucked in a breath, his arms tightening around her waist. 'Christ, yes.'

'Well, I…' She undulated again, exaggerating the move, feeling a delicious tug below her belly button as the raw emotion receded and the thrum of her pulse took its place. 'Would not.' Loosening her arms, she glanced down, searching his gaze. 'I'm going to need to apologise in advance because I don't think this is going to take very long.'

'Are you kidding? If you think I'm going to last more than a second or two longer than you do, then you are seriously underestimating what you do to me.'

Chelsea's heart skipped. Aaron Vincent was *seriously* pushing all her buttons.

She dropped her head then and kissed him, slow at first, then faster and hungrier as his mouth demanded it, his tongue flicking against hers. The fever of her desperation flamed anew and she felt an answering flare in him, *heard* it echoed in the heavy rasp of his breathing. Two large hands slid to her buttocks and squeezed and Chelsea rocked then, setting up a rhythm.

'God...*yes*.' Aaron groaned against her lips as he squeezed harder.

She rocked more but it wasn't enough. Chelsea pushed at Aaron's chest, breaking their kiss. 'Lie back,' she commanded huskily.

Aaron eased back against the windscreen, his hands sliding to her hips, and Chelsea took a moment to admire his big shoulders and his smooth chest and the solid abs that clearly stayed honed from hefting around sheep. She rocked again, her movements freer this time, getting off on the hiss of his breath and the way those abdominals pulled taut.

'God, Chelsea...' He shook his head as his eyes roamed from her face to her breasts to the flare of her hips and to where they were joined, before drifting up again. 'I've never seen anything as beautiful as you with diamonds in your hair riding me into the night.'

Chelsea's heart squeezed hard at the hushed compliment. The awe in his voice humbled her with its intensity and she realised she could fall in love with this man.

And it didn't scare the living daylights out of her.

Sliding a hand onto his stomach, Chelsea felt the ripple of his muscles beneath. Felt every ripple as the other hand joined in and they smoothed their way up to his pecs and then on to his shoulders, her palms grabbing onto their solid roundness. She leaned forward into her extended arms, the position changing the angle of their joining. His hand clutched convulsively at her hip and she shivered as it hit just the right spot.

Staring at each other, he withdrew a little

then thrust, and Chelsea moaned and shut her eyes as it felt *so* good. He did it again and it rocked her breasts and her head, and her sex clenched around him. When he went again, she rose to meet his withdrawal and fell to heighten his thrust. He grunted and she gasped, her eyes flying open, their gazes connecting.

They moved together then, just like that, eyes locked, Chelsea leaning into her palms as she rose and fell, Aaron's fingers biting into her hips as he thrust in and out, blood surging and pounding through her belly and buttocks and thighs, every nerve stretching taut, every muscle tightening, ripples of pleasure starting deep inside her sex.

'Oh, God… *Aaron*.'

'I know,' he panted, his eyes boring into hers as he went deeper and deeper with each thrust. 'I know, I know.'

The ripples got bigger and harder and faster until they exploded into an all-consuming deluge. Chelsea cried out, panting and gasping, her eyes wide as a tide of sensation swept her away. 'Oh, God.' Her nails dug into his shoulders as her body trembled with the first pulses of her orgasm. 'Yes, yes, yes.'

As promised, Aaron joined her in the torrent two beats later, shouting his release into the night. *'Chelsea!'*

He vaulted up then, taking her with him, his hands sliding around high on her back, his fingers anchoring from behind on the balls of her shoulders, holding her close as he kissed her, locking her in their starry, starry night together. Stealing her breath and giving her his own, he kissed up the tumult, bucking and shuddering, his climax sustaining hers until the last tremor rocked her core.

Chelsea's mouth left his, her chin coming to rest on top of his head, his lips buzzing her throat as she caught her breath.

'That was…' he said, his breathing still unsteady.

Chelsea waited for him to continue and, when he didn't, she laughed. He sounded satisfied and mystified all at once, as if he couldn't come up with an adequate enough word, and hell if that didn't set up a warm glow in her heart. 'Yeah. I know.'

Chuckling, he eased back, taking her with him, cradling her against his chest, making her excruciatingly aware of how intimately they were still joined. The steady bang of his heart echoed under her ear as his fingers trekked idly up and down the furrow of her spine, and they lay there for several minutes, just breathing in the aftermath.

'You okay?' he asked eventually.

'Mmm,' she said. 'I haven't felt this okay in a long time.'

His arms squeezed around her, and Chelsea snuggled for a beat or two more, but with the night still warm she was conscious of the sweat slicking between them. She roused and pushed up, making to move off him, only to have his hand clamp on her arse.

'Not yet,' he murmured, his gaze settling on hers.

'I'm too heavy,' she protested.

He gave a snort-laugh. 'Half the sheep I moved today weighed more than you.' But he lifted his hand and Chelsea eased away. She shivered and a low kind of hum came from the back of his throat as he slid from her body.

She settled against the windscreen, her knees bent as Aaron sat and ditched the condom before zipping up. Chelsea supposed she should try and find her dress, but then he was beside her again, his hand slipping into hers, and the thought floated away.

Neither of them spoke for a long time. Somehow, the stars seemed even brighter now, and it was lovely lying here with Aaron

under that sky with the memory of their joining lingering in the still night air.

'I hear you can see the aurora down here.'

'Aurora Australis. Yes. But not out here…
Gotta go further south. You can see them
in Victoria sometimes on a good night, but
Tassie's the best place.'

'Have you been to Tasmania?'

'When I was a kid.'

'I'd like to see the southern lights in Tasmania some time,' she murmured, her eyes
roaming the sky.

'I would, too. Maybe…' He turned his
head. 'We could go together?'

Conscious of his gaze on her profile, Chelsea also turned her head. 'I'd like that.'

When he smiled, she smiled back before
she returned her gaze to the sky in time to
catch a shooting star flaring across the se-
quined black dome above. She gasped and
pointed at it, her finger following its trajec-
tory.

'You get to make a wish now,' he said.

'Nope.' Her lips curved into a smile. 'I
think I've been lucky enough for one night.'

'Amen to that,' he murmured.

Chelsea laughed at his deadpan delivery
and rolled up onto her elbow, looking down
into his smiling face. The starlight fell gently

on the crinkles around his eyes, the crooked smile and the slight asymmetry of his eyes.

'How'd you do this?' she asked, her finger tracing the uneven line of his nose.

'Footy,' he said. 'Two broken noses.'

'And this?' Her finger brushed over the asymmetrical bow of his top lip.

'Fractured zygoma. Also footy.' He laughed, as if everyone who played the game ended up with broken noses and cheekbones. 'Didn't quite heal in perfect symmetry so my face has always looked a bit crooked.'

Chelsea drifted her finger over the cheekbone in question before drifting it back to his top lip. 'I like your crooked face,' she murmured.

She liked it a lot.

He smiled and his hand came up to capture hers, their gazes locking as he kissed her fingertips, and Chelsea's lungs felt too big for her chest. How could she have all these feelings for him so soon? It had taken her months to fall in love with Dom.

Before she blurted anything else out, she snuggled down beside him—as much as one could snuggle against glass—her head on his shoulder, her arm across his chest, her fingers absently caressing a nicely pillowed pectoral muscle.

It was so damned quiet out here. Had she been alone, she might have found all this vast black emptiness eerie, but with Aaron it felt…intimate.

'You know,' he said after a while, his fingers drifting up and down her arm, 'I still have my bedroom at the homestead.'

Chelsea's fingers stopped their caress. Stay the night at the homestead? Did he mean sneak in and sneak out again before morning? Or just go on back and not care who saw them?

It was tempting, but part of her shied away from that kind of public declaration. This *thing* was some*thing*. And that was big—for both of them. Except it had just happened, and she couldn't help but feel it would be easier to figure out without the speculation, scrutiny and expectation of family and friends.

'Too soon?'

Chelsea let out a shaky breath. 'Yeah.' Pushing up onto her elbow again, her gaze found his. 'Is that okay?'

'Of course.' Levering himself up, Aaron kissed her lightly, briefly. 'Come on. I'll drop you back to your place.'

'Drop me?' Her index finger traced the

crooked line of his top lip. 'I was hoping you might stay.'

He raised an eyebrow, his mouth lifting beneath the pad of her finger into an answering smile. 'I thought it was too early.'

God…this man was just too damned sweet and considerate, but Chelsea didn't want this night to end. 'For your place, sure. Not for mine.'

She grinned at him and he grinned back.

CHAPTER NINE

THREE WEEKS LATER, Chelsea was with Travis and Aaron at a large community health clinic set up under the shade of some towering gums a few hundred kilometres north of Balanora. The morning was hot, as per usual, but there was some cloud cover and a light breeze helping to keep things bearable.

It had been the most blissful three weeks of her life. Bliss hadn't been a state she'd thought she'd ever occupy again, but laughing and talking over takeaway and Netflix, followed by long, steamy nights in bed—thank God for air-conditioning—and sexy lie-ins on shared days off was pretty damn close to nirvana.

The fact they were keeping it to themselves gave it a little extra spice.

Some might call it sneaking around but Chelsea preferred the term 'discretion'. And Aaron was fully on board with keeping things quiet for a while so she just relaxed and enjoyed it. She had thought it might make working together awkward but, compared to their original awkwardness over that hotel barge-in and her snatched kiss, this was nothing and they soon learned to cultivate their at-work personas.

And Chelsea was pretty sure they'd pulled it off. Until today.

Blowing away her third sticky fly in a minute, she administered a vaccine to her patient in one arm while Travis took her blood pressure on the other. Sadie was a well-known indigenous elder and artist in the region, and spritely for her seventy-eight years, given her arthritic knees and partial blindness in her left eye.

'Gotta hand it to you, Chels,' Travis said, his Santa hat sitting rakishly on his head. With Christmas less than a week away, they were all wearing one. Even Hattie, who was currently kicking a ball around with some kids. 'It's been almost seven weeks and you've managed to avoid saying *bloody flies*. Didn't think you had it in you.'

Chelsea slid a glance at Aaron, who was bent over Jasmine, Sadie's great-granddaughter, stethoscope hanging down from his neck as he performed her six-week postnatal check. A smile touched his mouth but he didn't look up from the baby.

Sadie glanced at her, then at Aaron, then at Travis as he ripped off the blood pressure cuff. She cocked her eyebrow at him. 'They're doing it, right?'

Chelsea glanced at Sadie, alarmed, as Travis nodded. 'We're pretty sure. We're taking bets back at the base on when they'll make it official.'

Bets? Her cheeks grew hot as she stuck a plaster over the vaccination site. Sadie hooted out a laugh and slapped her thigh, her snowy-white hair flicking around her face as Chelsea snuck another look at Aaron. He was clearly biting his cheek to stop from smiling.

'They're playing things close to their chest,' Travis said. 'But Siobhan saw Aaron skulking—'

'I don't skulk,' he interrupted, not looking up as he gently pushed on the infant's adducted hips to check for dysplasia.

'Skulking,' Travis continued, 'down Chelsea's front path at quarter to eight at night two weeks ago with a bag of Chinese takeaway from the Happy Sun in his hand. And when I asked them both at work the next day what they had for dinner, he said beef and black bean and she said…' he paused for dramatic effect '…a cheese toasty.'

Chelsea remembered that incident. As soon as Aaron had said Chinese, she'd known she couldn't say that too in case it roused suspicion. So, she'd panicked and said the other.

'What?' Sadie shook her head dismissively. 'No one has a toasted sanger when you can have Happy Sun.'

Travis leaned in conspiratorially. 'I know, right?'

'Yep.' She glanced at Chelsea then at Aaron. 'They're doing it.'

That was their evidence? 'We're right here, you know!' Chelsea said as she tossed the empty syringe into the nearby sharps container.

'Reckon it'll last?' Sadie continued, ignoring Chelsea's statement.

'We hope so.' Travis grinned at Chelsea. 'We like her.'

Pursing her lips, Sadie inspected them both again, before returning her attention to Travis. 'Yeah. Reckon it will.'

'From your lips to God's ears, Aunty.'

Sadie narrowed her eyes at Aaron. 'About time, boy.' Clearly, Sadie and Aaron had known each other for a long time.

'No comment,' he said, unperturbed.

Chelsea shut her eyes. No comment meant yes—everyone knew that. Another hoot of laughter escaped the old woman's lips. '*Definitely* doing it.'

They were back in the plane three hours later, having done over fifty different vaccinations, a dozen infant health checks, some post-hospital admission follow-up and seen to miscellaneous other things, from a festered splinter to a mild burn to a case of shingles. Chelsea was buckled into her usual seat, diagonally opposite and facing Aaron. They were waiting for Travis.

'No comment?' she murmured into the mouthpiece as she switched over to a private channel.

He just shrugged and smiled. 'It was bound to get out sooner or later. Is that a problem?'

Chelsea expected to feel hesitancy. Doubt. Uncertainty. But there was none forthcoming. She realised she'd been worried about what people—both in Balanora and back in London—would say about how quick it had been. But, maybe that wasn't *her* problem.

Slowly, she shook her head. 'No, actually.'

He smiled his crooked smile and the slight tension she didn't know had been there seemed to melt from around his shoulders before her eyes. 'Why don't we talk about it tonight?' he suggested.

'Yeah,' she said, and smiled too. They'd been avoiding having a conversation about the future. Or maybe *she* had. But her feelings for Aaron weren't going away, and what was she afraid of exactly? That Aaron would turn out to be like Dom? That he'd cheat?

She'd known him for less than two months and already she could tell he was nothing like Dom. Hell, she'd been able to tell that the second she'd rashly kissed him in her house and he'd stepped away. *He'd* called a halt.

Just then Travis made his way down the aisle, adjusting his headphones. Chelsea feigned interest in looking out of the window as she flicked the channel back to a shared one. So did Aaron.

Travis shook his head. 'You two are so damn cute,' he muttered in their ears. 'Don't keep us in suspense for too much longer.'

Hattie's voice said, 'Amen.'

Aaron's mood was buoyant when they landed just before one in the afternoon. He and Chelsea were going to talk and they'd had a great day out at the clinic. He absolutely loved getting to the outer reaches of the district. He might be the doctor but people didn't treat him any differently than they had when he'd been a boy.

Sadie was a classic example. He'd played in the same footy team as a lot of Sadie's grandkids and assorted other relatives, and she'd always been on the side lines, no matter where they'd played, a staunch supporter of the team. She'd always been the first one to clap and say, 'Good tackle,' or 'Great try,' but also the first to tell him to pull his head in if he gave the ref any lip or if she felt he was getting too big for his footy boots.

'Don't need no prima donnas out here, boy,' she'd say.

It didn't surprise him that she'd twigged to what was going on between Chelsea and him. He swore the old people—the women in particular—knew what he was thinking even before he did. It felt a lot like having a mother, and perhaps that was what the women out in these small communities, proudly living on their country were—his mothers. Closing ranks after his mum had split, filling that gap, poking and prodding him to do better, be better.

The fact Sadie seemed to approve of the situation with Chelsea said a lot about the type of woman Chelsea was. Inherently suspicious of newcomers, ingrained into generations of old people who had seen too much sadness and grief in their lives, Sadie didn't just take to anyone. But she'd been joking and teasing, and if that wasn't a stamp of approval then he didn't know what was.

Having Chelsea seem pretty zen about being outed had been the icing on the cake.

So, despite himself, Aaron started to hope. He'd told her in the beginning that he didn't get involved with out-of-towners, and how much more out-of-town could a woman from *London* be? But back then he'd thought she was still in love with Dom, and they hadn't spent weeks together laughing and eating and sharing.

And *talking.* About going to Tasmania, and other places he'd suggested they could go to together. Talking about her being in Balanora next year and the year after.

Aaron knew how he felt. He was in love with her. It was that simple. And that complex. But, these past few weeks, he'd started to think that she felt the same way, or that she might be starting to, anyway. Maybe he was just a giant fool, but her willingness to talk about their relationship—there, *he* was labelling it—only filled him with more hope.

* * *

As they were the last two to disembark the plane, Chelsea leered at him cheekily on her way out. Glancing at the swish of her ponytail and the perky little stab of her pen, Aaron made a quick grab for her hand, pulling her back and toppling her onto his lap. She gave a little squeak as she landed.

'Aaron!' she protested on a whisper, laughing as she tried to squirm out of his grasp. 'Trent could come back.'

'I don't care,' he muttered.

It was clear everyone pretty much knew anyway, and that not only made him happy but exceptionally turned on. Keeping his hands to himself around her was difficult at the best of times, but suddenly the possibility of a *them* loomed large, and the urge to kiss the hell out of her beat like a mantra through his blood.

She melted against him the second his mouth touched hers, kissing him back with equal abandon. 'Ever heard of the mile-high club?' he murmured a minute later, coming up for some air.

Laughing, she said, 'We're on the ground.'

A loud knock on the fuselage followed by Trent's stern, 'Don't make me bring a blue light in there,' had them both laughing.

Aaron rubbed his nose against Chelsea's. 'Tonight,' he whispered, and her contented sigh was better than any quickie in an aeroplane loo.

'Can't wait.'

But those plans were dashed about thirty seconds after they deplaned. 'Sorry, Chels,' Charmaine said as she met them at the entrance to the hangar, 'but we've had several phone calls from a Roberto Rossi asking for you.'

She frowned. 'Roberto?'

'He said he'd left you several messages, but I explained that you were in an area with no mobile coverage. He wouldn't say what he wanted but he asked that you ring him urgently and that you knew the number.'

A prickle flared at Aaron's nape as Chelsea delved in her pocket, retrieving her phone and switching it on. Nobody ever had their mobiles on when they went out. They couldn't have it on in the plane, and there was rarely any mobile coverage in the places they went anyway.

Aaron could see what looked like at least a dozen missed-call notifications on her screen as she tapped the first one and put the phone to her ear. He wasn't sure if he should go and give her some privacy, but she hadn't asked him or Charmaine to leave, nor had she walked away, and he didn't want to dessert her in case it was bad news and she needed someone to lean on.

Him, hopefully.

Her brow furrowed further as she listened to what he assumed was one of the messages before she pulled the phone away from her ear and tapped to end the call.

'Is everything okay?' Charmaine asked, getting in before Aaron, who was trying to read her body language, could say a word.

She shook her head as she glanced at Aaron. 'It's Alfie.'

Charmaine frowned this time. 'Is that a niece or a nephew?'

'Yeah.' Chelsea nodded. 'Something like that.'

'What happened?' Aaron asked, moving closer, not touching her but wanting to. Wanting to slip his hand onto her neck or an arm around her waist and hating that he couldn't.

'I don't know, it was pretty garbled. He's in Intensive Care.' She turned to Charmaine. 'Do you mind if I use the phone in your office to ring Roberto back?'

'Of course not.'

Charmaine squeezed her arm and Aaron wished he could do the same. But suddenly he felt very uncertain about where they stood. Her dead husband's child, a child who had *wormed his way into her heart*, was in Intensive Care.

Would she go back? To London. To *home*. The place she knew, where people loved her and most of her stuff was still stored.

And would she return to Balanora?

He felt like all kinds of bastard to be worried about himself in a moment like this, but everything he'd felt less than a minute ago was disintegrating around him, and he wasn't at all sure he'd get it back.

Chelsea placed her hand over top of Charmaine's and returned her squeeze. 'Thanks,' she said before dropping her hand and hurrying across the hangar.

They watched her as she disappeared through the door to the offices. 'You okay?' Charmaine asked, turning to face him.

Aaron gave a snort as he looked at her. 'Am I that transparent?'

Her mouth curved into a gentle smile. 'I've known you a long time.'

'I...love her.'

'That was...' Charmaine paused, as if searching for the right word. 'Fast.'

'Seems like it runs in my family.'

'No.' She shook her head. 'Your mother

was a city girl who came here pregnant and always had one eye on the highway.'

'She lives in London, Char.'

'No, Aaron. She lives *here*. She's inordinately qualified. She could have got a job in any of the big capital cities, but she *chose* here. And she's made more effort in the short time she's been here to be part of this community then your mum did in fifteen years. She came to a bloody CWA meeting with me three days ago.'

The Country Women's Association was a service organisation that formed the backbone of any Outback community. His mother had referred to them as the 'blue rinse set'.

'She's going to want to go back.' Aaron wished he didn't know that already, but the sinking feeling in the pit of his stomach said otherwise. Because, as much as Chelsea had wanted out of the situation back home, she was deeply compassionate. He doubted she could turn away from people who had been—*were*—a huge part of her life in their hour of need.

'Okay.' Charmaine nodded. 'We'll work it out.'

'And if she doesn't return?'

She raised her eyebrow. 'Are you that unlovable?'

No, it wasn't that. 'It's new.'

Charmaine gave his arm the same squeeze she'd given to Chelsea. 'Have some faith.' Dropping her hand, she said, 'C'mon, let's go see what she needs.'

By the time they were back in the office, Chelsea was hanging up the phone at Charmaine's desk. Aaron knocked quietly on the door, pushing it gently open. She looked pale and he knew the news wasn't good.

'What happened?'

'He ran out on the road to get his ball. A car knocked him over. He has a fractured skull and a bleed on the brain. It sounds like it's small enough to manage conservatively because they're not talking surgery. Roberto's in shock, so he didn't know a lot of other information. He had a seizure at the scene so he's on a vent and he also has a broken tib-fib.'

'Bloody hell.' That was some major trauma. Aaron moved closer, halting on the other side of the desk. He wanted to hug her but he was conscious of their lack of privacy. 'Is he stable?'

'I think. For now.' She shrugged. 'Roberto was very upset. Francesca was looking after him. She's apparently inconsolable. I...' She paused, placing a hand on her stomach as if she was quelling nausea. 'I have to go.'

Aaron ignored the giant fist ramming straight into his gut and the slick edge of his own nausea as he accepted that this was probably the end of the road for them.

Damn it, *why* had he left himself hope?

'Of course.' He nodded. 'The afternoon flight leaves at four. You could be on that.'

It cost him to slip into organisational mode but the last thing she needed right now was him being whiny about what Alfie's potentially life-threatening condition meant for them. For *him*. She needed him to be a god damned man and step up.

Her shoulders sagged a little. 'There's usually a few flights to London around nine out of Brisbane.'

Charmaine entered and joined him at the desk. 'Why don't you go home, have a shower, grab what you need and I'll get Meg to book the flights? She has all your passport and preference details.'

'Oh, no.' Chelsea shook her head. 'I can do all that.'

'Nonsense. Meg organises flights all the time—it's a huge part of her job. And she's a bloody whizz at it. She'll find the best value last-minute, most direct flight she can.'

'But I'll need to pay…'

Charmaine waved her hand dismissively. 'We'll worry about that later. You just go to your family.'

'But…' Chelsea glanced at Aaron then back to Charmaine. 'I'm leaving you in the lurch.'

'It's fine.' Another dismissive wave. 'There are nurses at the hospital who can and do cover for us when we have a shortfall.'

Chelsea blinked. 'Thank you.'

Aaron moved to the door. 'I'll drive you home.'

'No.' She shook her head firmly. 'I'm fine. I don't need—' She stopped abruptly and shook her head before dropping her gaze. 'I'm fine.'

He stiffened. He could fill in the blanks just fine. She didn't need him. 'Of course.' He took a steadying breath. 'Safe travels.'

She nodded then glanced at Charmaine. 'Thank you.' And then she was pushing away from the desk, slowing as she neared where Aaron was standing in the doorway. 'I'll be back,' she said, looking at him now.

Aaron nodded, his throat as dry as the red Outback dirt. 'Yep,' he murmured, keeping his voice even and friendly.

Her hand slid over his and squeezed, her brown gaze locking on his. 'I *will* be back.'

And then she was gone leaving Aaron about as wretched as he'd ever felt, clinging to her words but not hopeful, despite the utter certainty of her tone. The thing he'd feared the most had come true—Chelsea was leaving—and there was a giant hole in his chest. He'd let his guard down, broken his own rule and fallen head-over-heels in love, like some damned sappy teenager, and now it was all going to hell.

And that was on him. Not her. Because he'd known better.

Chelsea walked aimlessly around the shops in the forecourt of Brisbane international airport, waiting for check-in to open. She'd arrived at the international terminal from the domestic one not long after she'd got off her flight from Balanora. She was a few hours early, but there was no point leaving the terminal complex when the flight left at nine-thirty.

She had managed to get through to Great Ormond Street hospital and talk to the neurosurgeon in charge of Alfie's care, whom she'd worked with several years ago at another hospital. The news had improved, it seemed. Alfie's vitals were stable, he had woken and recognised his mother and they'd removed the ventilation. He was sleepy but there hadn't been any more seizures.

All encouraging signs.

The surgeon had stressed that the bleed was tiny and the skull fracture only hair-line, and had been cautiously optimistic. She knew, of course, things could turn on a dime, but it had settled the knot of nerves sitting like an oily lump in her stomach and freed up some headspace to think about Aaron.

About his neutral expression and the forced friendliness in his voice and the way his walls had come up before her eyes. The ones that had been there when he'd stepped back from her clumsy kiss at her house that first night, and in the store room when he'd said they were just going to be friends.

Before that magical night at Curran Downs. And all the ones since.

She'd tried to assure him she was coming back, but she could tell he hadn't believed her, and she hated that maybe she'd made him feel *not enough* by leaving. It wasn't a nice way to feel. But she hadn't been able to face him coming home with her, either. She didn't want him there with those walls in his eyes, watching her pack, taking her to the airport, wishing her a stiff goodbye.

Not to mention she wouldn't *want* to go. They'd have closed her door behind them, shut the world out and she'd have broken down and clung to him. She'd have cried at the unfairness of life and how this pocket of joy she'd found here in Balanora was being ripped out from under her…and what kind of a person did that make her when Alfie was in ICU?

Selfish. Callous. Heartless.

No, she had to do this by herself. Francesca and Roberto, who had already been through so much, needed her. And she'd figure out the rest as the next few days unfolded.

With thirty minutes to go until check-in opened, Chelsea found a quiet corner in a café and ordered a coffee. It had just arrived when her mobile rang—Roberto.

Answering it immediately, she said, '*Ciao*, Roberto.'

'No, Chelsea, it's me,' Francesca said. 'I'm using Roberto's phone.'

'Francesca, how are you?'

She broke down in tears and Chelsea spent the next five minutes soothing and calming her, assuring her she hadn't done anything wrong, that accidents happened, and encouraging her to see the positives in Alfie's condition.

'Thank you so much for coming, Chelsea. Dom would want you to be with us.'

Chelsea gritted her teeth. Not that long ago the mention of Dom's name would have tugged on all her emotional strings, served up with a hefty dose of guilt because she couldn't keep loving him the way his parents clearly wanted her to.

Not so any more.

She wanted to say, *You didn't know Dom. I didn't know Dom.* But Francesca was distressed enough, so Chelsea cut her some slack.

'This is what I was afraid of. Something bad happening after you left, and it's come true.'

Grinding her teeth now, Chelsea took a steadying breath. Francesca was stressed and feeling guilty about Alfie's accident. She *would* cut her slack, damn it. 'It's just coincidence,' Chelsea soothed, well used to this role with her mother-in-law who, despite being born and raised in a third-generation English household, could lean heavily into her Italian *mamma* roots.

'At least you'll be home for Christmas. That's good.'

Christmas. Chelsea's stomach sank.

'Roberto tells me you changed your name back to Tanner but...why, Chelsea? How could you do that to us?' she chided. 'To Dom. Reject his name. Betray him like that just three years after he was put in the ground.'

Chelsea blinked. Okay. *No.* A red mist blurred her vision. She was officially out of slack. Francesca had to be freaking kidding.

'Betray *him*?' Chelsea didn't even recognise her own voice as she gripped the phone.

'Chelsea. Come on now.'

'Betray *him*?' she repeated.

'We don't speak ill of the dead.'

She didn't have to be there to know that Francesca was probably crossing herself. 'He betrayed *me*, Francesca.' Her hand shook and she wrapped it around her coffee cup. 'He *betrayed* me. He slept with another woman and got her pregnant.'

It was on the tip of Chelsea's tongue to unload about the other women too, but she couldn't let the rage storming through her system destroy everything in its path. She would only regret it later.

'Chelsea, *bella*, women always threw themselves at him. You know that. He was such a good-looking boy.'

Chelsea barely bit back her gasp. 'Francesca!' Several people nearby turned to look at her as her voice whipped from her throat. 'Your son *cheated* on me.' She lowered her voice but there was no mistaking the edge of fury. 'He took our vow of fidelity and he stomped all over it and there is no excuse for that. *None*. He can hide from the responsibility of that in death, but I won't let you hide from the truth of it or pretend he was some kind of saint any more. I had to spend the last year in Hackney seeing the woman he betrayed me with and their child almost every day. Do you understand how much that *hurt*? Do you have *any* idea?'

She drew a shaky breath. Every part of her trembled. She'd never spoken to her mother-in-law like this but this was her line in the sand.

No more Saint Dom.

'Dom was my husband and, yes, I loved him. But he *hurt* me and that changed everything. Sure, he was human and he was flawed, and neither of us can go back and change what he did. But *I* can change how *I* feel. And I don't love him any more, Francesca.'

She loved Aaron. Yes—*she loved Aaron*.

A rush of emotion swamped Chelsea's chest as quiet sobbing sounded in her ear, and she sat with the truth of her feelings, growing and glowing, giving her courage not to take back every word in the face of Francesca's tears. It felt as if a yoke had been ripped from her neck and Chelsea wouldn't pick it up and put it back on again.

Dom was her past. Aaron was her future.

'I'm sorry, Chelsea,' Francesca said eventually as her weeping subsided. 'I didn't understand. You were always so good and kind about it, I underestimated how much having Krystal and Alfie around hurt you. How much *Dom* hurt you. I'm so, so sorry.'

Breathing out slowly, Chelsea's chest filled with a different kind of emotion. For the first time since Alfie had arrived on the scene, she actually felt as though Francesca *really* understood how difficult the last year had been for her, and the shackles that had kept them joined together in a cycle of grief and guilt fell away. Which made her next decision even easier.

'I'm not coming, Francesca.'

'Chelsea…please, *bella*.'

She was so used to being the one that Francesca and Roberto relied on since Dom's death, it was strange to realise that they'd be okay without her. They had plenty of family—they'd always had plenty of family. And now it was time to lean on them.

She was drawing a line in the sand.

Charmaine had told her to go to her family, and for a long time Hackney and the Rossis had been her family. More so than the house she'd grown up in. But things happened, feelings altered, directions changed. And, even though she'd been in Balanora for such a short period of time, when she thought of family she thought of that hangar baking under the Outback sun in the middle of nowhere.

She thought of Charmaine and Hattie and Travis. She thought of *Aaron*.

'It's time, Francesca. Krystal and Alfie need you, and Roberto and the rest of the family. They don't need me.' Francesca had been trying hard to hang on with both hands but it was time to let go. 'You've got to let me live my life now.'

There were more quiet tears, but when Francesca next spoke she said, 'You will keep in touch, won't you?'

'Of course. I'm not cutting you out of my life, and I want to keep across Alfie's progress. We're just…turning a new page.'

'You like it there?'

Chelsea smiled. 'I *love* it here.'

Five minutes later, with her carry-on bag rolling behind her—her only piece of luggage—Chelsea strode out into the Brisbane sunshine.

The next morning, just after eleven, and almost seven weeks to the day she'd first landed in Balanora, Chelsea was back. It was still scorching hot as she walked off the plane and onto the Tarmac but she barely noticed. She only had one thing on her mind as she got into the nearest taxi—go to Aaron.

He had a couple of days off now and she knew he'd planned to go to Curran Downs because she'd been going with him. A quick phone call to the house phone confirmed that he'd arrived there last night and had gone straight to the river to camp for a couple of days.

So, the river it was.

Chelsea was home for five minutes—just long enough to divest herself of her suitcase and get into that green strappy dress he liked so much. Then she was in her car and heading to Curran Downs. She'd been there three times now, so she knew the way, but the trip felt ten times longer, her anxiety growing more acute as her car ate up the miles.

What if she'd blown it? What if she'd permanently damaged things between them by her abrupt departure?

When she reached the homestead, Tracey was waiting for her with a four-wheel-drive vehicle. Even though Aaron had taken her to the river last time she'd been to Curran Downs, it was a slightly more complicated path, and Tracey had suggested on the phone that she drop Chelsea there and she and Aaron could come back in Aaron's vehicle when they were ready.

'Is everything okay with Alfie?' Tracey asked as she gave Chelsea a quick hug.

'Yep. Off life-support. Talking. Not quite his usual chatty self but apparently doing well.' She'd checked in with Great Ormond Street and Francesca this morning before her flight to Balanora.

'A good outcome.'

Chelsea nodded. 'Yes.'

'Get in,' Tracey said in her typical no-nonsense way, which suited Chelsea just fine.

She had no desire to swap pleasantries— she just needed to find Aaron. They needed to talk. And she needed to feel his arms around her.

Any other time, Chelsea would have enjoyed the drive. The vast canvas of the Outback topped off by a bright-blue sky was magnificent in that grand sweeping way of all landscape vistas. But today she was too preoccupied to be appreciative of the scenery.

'Is Aaron okay?' she asked, staring out of the window at nothing, conscious only of her own heartbeat as they jostled along through the scrub.

'He's fine.'

She turned sharply. 'Really?'

Tracey glanced over. 'Aaron's not much of a talker,' she clarified as she returned her attention to the bush track.

'I screwed up.' Unfortunately, admitting it out loud didn't help any.

'But you're here to fix it, right?'

'Yes.' A thousand times yes.

'Well, then…'

'What if it's too late?'

Tracey laughed. It wasn't cruel or unkind, merely amused. 'You've been gone one day.'

'That's long enough for regret to set in.'

'Nah.' Tracey shook his head. 'Aaron's not built like that. Our mother leaving taught him to guard his heart, sure. But, unlike me, it also taught him how to forgive, and how to understand that this place isn't for everyone, and that's actually not some horrible kind of flaw.'

Tracey's mouth tilted upwards and Chelsea

smiled at his sister's self-deprecation, despite the niggle of anxiety pecking at her brain. 'It's for me,' Chelsea said.

This vast expanse of red dirt and blue sky, so different from where she had come from, had worked its way under her skin. Just as Aaron had.

'Good.' She nodded. 'Tell him that.'

Twenty minutes later, Aaron's ute came into view, parked under the shade of some river gums. Chelsea spotted him sitting on the back tray, a frosty bottle in his hand, the same time he heard the engine, craning his neck in its direction. She could see his brows knit together as he tried to figure out why his sister was here, and who was in the passenger seat, and she clocked the second he realised it was her, his expression briefly surprised before turning guarded.

He leapt off the back of the ute as Tracey pulled her vehicle up alongside his. She put the window down but kept the engine running. 'Brought you a visitor,' she said with a smile.

Chelsea swallowed as Aaron looked at her as if she was some kind of mirage. His eyes ate her up as hers did him. It had been less than twenty-four hours but she'd *missed* him. Missed his crooked face and his carelessly messy hair swooping across his forehead. Missed the way he filled out a T-shirt and shorts.

Missed the way he looked at her as though she was special. As though she was *enough*.

A trill of anticipation caused her hand to tremble as she placed it on the door handle and pushed. Chelsea's pulse fluttered at her temple and she wondered if she'd ever stop feeling as though she'd been plugged into an electrical socket when he was near.

She hoped not.

'Thanks, Tracey,' she said as she slid out of the four-wheel drive, the heat hitting hard after the frigid air-con in the cab.

'No worries,' Tracey replied cheerfully, then winked at her brother as Chelsea shut the door and stood clear. 'You kiddies behave now, you hear.'

She drove off then, but neither of them really noticed as they stood staring at each other for long moments. 'Chelsea?' There was so much hope in his voice as he took a step forward, then his brow furrowed and he halted. 'Is Alfie…? Did he…? He didn't…?'

'No.' She shook her head. 'He's fine, doing well. Off the vent, stable GCS, in a stepdown ward. The fracture was hairline and the bleed quite small. They're confident it should resolve reasonably quickly and he should make a full recovery in time.'

He breathed on a rush. 'That's so good. Everyone must be very relieved.'

'Yeah. They'll feel better when he's home but they're counting their blessings.'

'So, you…' He eyed her speculatively and she swore she saw hope in his eyes. 'Didn't get on the plane?'

She smiled as she shook her head slowly. 'I did not.'

'Because Alfie's condition had improved?'

'Not because of that, no.'

'Okay.' He looked as though he wanted to come closer but shoved his hands on his hips instead. 'Because?'

Chelsea took a step towards him instead. 'I had an epiphany at the airport.'

'Oh.' He swallowed. 'You did, huh?'

'I did.'

'Care to share?'

Taking another step, Chelsea halted about three metres from him, aware suddenly of the volume of silence all around them. 'I realised that I wasn't responsible for Dom's family. And that it wasn't fair of them to expect me to keep playing the part of grieving widow.

That I needed to move on. That we all needed to move on.'

A beat or two passed between them then Aaron took a tentative step in her direction. 'That sounds…healthy.'

Chelsea nodded. The husky edge to his voice sounded strained. 'I also realised that I'd fallen in love with you.'

He blinked. 'You…did?'

'I know it's crazy, Aaron.' Her pulse was jumping all over the place as she inched closer to him. She was pretty sure he felt the same but he didn't seem to be leaping for joy at her admission. 'I know it's not been very long but…'

Within two strides he was grabbing her up and hauling her close, her breasts flattened against his chest, his hands cradling either side of her face as he kissed her—hard. Her pulse thrummed madly, the scent of the bush and the taste of beer filling her senses, making her dizzy.

'God,' he muttered, breaking away to kiss her eyes and her nose and nuzzle her temple, his fast, raspy breath ruffling her hair. 'I didn't think you'd come back.'

Chelsea's breathing was equally as erratic. 'I'm sorry, I'm so sorry I left so quickly, I just panicked and reacted without thinking things through properly.' She shut her eyes as his lips caused all kinds of havoc. 'But I always planned on coming back. Always.'

'I thought the pull of home would be too much when you got there.' His lips trekked down the side of her face. 'With everything familiar that you knew and loved at your fingertips again. And I've been sitting here, kicking myself one moment for being such an idiot to fall for you, and planning on moving to the UK the next.'

Chelsea blinked. '*What?* Moving to the UK?'

'Of course. If it means being with you? Absolutely.'

She drew back, needing to make eye contact. Needing him to know. 'There's no need for that. *This* is my home now.' Her gaze captured his and locked. 'Balanora. And you. *You're* my home. I love you, Aaron, and I swear I'll never leave you like that again. *Never.* I think we've both spent a lot of our lives feeling like we weren't enough for people, but now we get to be each other's enough, and that's all I want. Just you and me for ever.'

'That's what I want too.' He kissed her again quickly, as if to assure her. 'I love you, Chelsea Tanner…and I know I've said this before, but you are *more* than enough. You are my everything. I am yours, and *only* yours, for ever and always.'

And that was all she needed. This man loving her in the same way she loved him—as big and as vast and as fathomless as the landscape around them.

For ever and always.

EPILOGUE

One year later, Christmas morning

CHELSEA STARED OUT of the window of the King Air as it made its descent to the graded red earth of the community airstrip below. Just beyond the strip, behind a low, tinsel-emblazoned partition, stood a gaggle of cheering kids, their eyes squinting expectantly at the approaching plane.

She was excited to be part of the annual Christmas Express run by the OA, which involved hopping from community to community on Christmas day, distributing gifts to kids in isolated areas and giving every child a chance to have a photo with Santa. It was one of the highlights of the OA calendar and Chelsea had been looking forward to it. Last year she'd been on call, and therefore unable to take part, but not this year!

She glanced across at Aaron as Hattie

landed the plane with her usual light touch. He was dressed in a red Santa suit, complete with snowy beard and a pillow for his belly, and Chelsea laughed as the plane taxied. 'Have I told you how hot you look in that suit?' she said into the headphone mic.

Santa might not usually be considered a sex symbol but it sure worked on Aaron.

'You look pretty hot too, elf girl.'

Chelsea blew him a kiss. She'd bought the elf suit online a few months ago when Charmaine had asked her what she wanted to dress up as for the Express. Seeing Aaron's face in the office this morning when she'd changed into it just prior to boarding, she was very pleased she had. The skirt was shortish and flirty, and the top, with the addition of a push-up bra, showed off a hint of cleavage.

It wasn't overtly sexy but he'd obviously liked what he saw and had whispered to her, 'You better wear that to bed tonight,' as he'd passed her by.

Thinking about it now, her heart overflowed anew with the depth of her feelings for this man who had filled her life this past year with so much love and joy. She couldn't remember ever being this happy. Their relationship had gone from strength to strength, and they'd moved in together six months ago.

Three months ago, they'd spent two fantastic weeks in Tasmania, including one glorious night witnessing the spectacle and majesty of the aurora.

And now this. Christmas day playing Santa in the Outback. Pinch her!

Alfie, who had made a full recovery, had been impressed when she'd told him she was flying with Santa today, and she'd promised him a picture of her with the man himself.

The plane came to a halt and Chelsea removed her headphones, unbuckling and springing up from her seat, eager to get outside, the bell on the end of her jaunty elf hat tinkling as she scooped up the Polaroid camera.

It was Aaron's turn to laugh. 'Having fun?' he teased as he pulled his headphones off and reached for the sack in front of him, neatly labelled by Meg as being for this stop.

She grinned, her heart full of love and Christmas spirit. 'Santa baby, this is the best time I've ever had.'

He shook his head slowly, his gaze capturing hers. '*You're* the best time I've ever had, Chelsea Tanner.'

Chelsea's insides melted to goo. The man said the sweetest damned things. *All the time.* 'Merry Christmas,' she murmured.

'Merry Christmas,' he replied. 'Here's to many more.'

Then, from a pocket, he produced some plastic mistletoe, held it up high with one hand and snagged her closer with the other, kissing her in a very un-Santa-like way.

Yes, Chelsea thought on a sigh. *Here's to many, many more.*

* * * * *

If you enjoyed this story, check out these other great reads from Amy Andrews

Tempted by Mr. Off-Limits
A Christmas Miracle
Swept Away by the Seductive Stranger
200 Harley Street: The Tortured Hero

All available now!